In the Arms of a Soldier

For A Soldier, the Nation is Always First

In the Arms of a Soldier

For A Soldier,
the Nation is Always First

BUDDHABHUSHAN KUCHEKAR

PRABHAT
PRAKASHAN

Published by
PRABHAT PRAKASHAN PVT. LTD.
4/19 Asaf Ali Road,
New Delhi-110 002 (INDIA)
e-mail: prabhatbooks@gmail.com

ISBN 978-93-5562-340-9
IN THE ARMS OF A SOLDIER: FOR A SOLDIER, THE NATION IS ALWAYS FIRST
by Buddhabhushan Kuchekar

Edition
First, 2024

Price
₹ 350 (Rupees Three Hundred Fifty Only)

Printed at
SS Japan Art, Delhi

Description

The love story of Pranali and Vikrant was an unlikely one. Pranali was an ordinary girl from Mumbai, while Vikrant was a Para Commando Major from the army. Their paths crossed one day at Victoria Garden in Kolkata, and they were drawn to each other immediately. Despite coming from different worlds, they fell deeply in love and decided to get married.

However, fate had other plans. Just two days before their wedding, Vikrant was called away on a mission. He had to leave Pranali behind, with their love story left incomplete. The pain of separation was immense, and Pranali struggled to cope with the loneliness and the uncertainty of not knowing when Vikrant would return.

Despite the challenges, Pranali held onto the hope that one day Vikrant would come back to her. She remained steadfast in her love for him, praying for his safe return and dreaming of the day when they could finally be united and together again. Their love story may have been interrupted, but it was far from over.

Author's Note

As an author, it has been my greatest pleasure to bring to you my first novel, the love story of Pranali and Major Vikrant, a story that is both beautiful and poignant in its simplicity. 'IN THE ARMS OF A SOLDIER ' is a story about two individuals who come from very different worlds, but who find a connection that transcends all barriers.

At its core, this book is a celebration of love - the love between two people, the love of country and the love of duty. It is a story that explores the sacrifices made by our soldiers, the challenges they face, and the courage they show in the face of adversity. Through the eyes of our protagonist, Captain Vikrant, we get a glimpse of the hardships and the emotional toll that the life of a soldier can take.

However, this book is not just about the soldier's life, but also about the joys and sorrows of ordinary people. The character of Pranali represents the hopes, dreams, and aspirations of the common person, and her journey is as much a part of this story as Vikrant's.

I also wanted to take this opportunity to acknowledge the sacrifices and service of our brave soldiers who put their lives on the line every day to protect our country. This book is a small tribute to their courage and resilience, and to their unwavering dedication to duty.

I hope that through the pages of this book, readers will gain a greater appreciation for the sacrifices made by our soldiers, and the importance of the role they play in our society. It is my hope that this book will inspire readers to reflect on the value of love, friendship, and service, and to appreciate the sacrifices made by those who serve our country.

In writing this book, I have tried to stay true to the emotions and experiences of the people who inspired it. I have attempted to portray the human side of our soldiers and their families, and to show the impact of their lives on those around them.

Thank you for taking the time to read this book, and I hope it will be a meaningful and enjoyable experience for you.

Sincerely,

– Buddhabhushan Hanumant Kuchekar

❑

Prologue

October 2018, Andheri East, Mumbai,

Pranali sat nervously at a corner table in Janvaar Restaurant, located in the busy district of Andheri East. In the bustling surroundings of the restaurant, Pranali was enveloped in a sea of strangers, yet she felt strangely alone. Her life had become a complex web of emotions, and in this moment, she was at a crossroads, uncertain of the path she should take.

As she anxiously scanned the restaurant, her eyes locked onto a tall figure entering the eatery. He was dressed in a pair of black pants and a neatly pressed navy blue shirt. His glasses framed his eyes, and his clean-shaven appearance showcased a sense of professionalism. Every step he took exuded confidence and purpose.

This man was Dr. Sameer, a doctor by profession and the son of a friend of Pranali's father. Their families had harboured hopes of a lasting partnership between them, envisaging a future where Pranali and Sameer would find happiness together.

However, as Pranali sat there, awaiting his arrival, her heart was elsewhere. It was consumed by the memory of "HIM". She knew that her heart belonged to "HIM", and despite the expectations of her family and the presence of Dr. Sameer, Pranali yearned for the return of her true love.

In this moment, two worlds collided within Pranali. On one side, there was Dr. Sameer, a man with a promising future and the potential for a stable life together. On the other side, there was the girl with a broken heart, who longed for the return of the one person who had captured her soul.

Dr. Sameer sat in front of her and apologised for being late.

She smiled and replied, ‘It’s fine.’ She then turned to look at her fingers on her hands. Pranali hesitated to tell Dr. Sameer something, even though he knew she wanted to. Given that it was their first meeting, he wanted her to feel at ease.

‘What would you like to order?’ he asked, his voice warm with a hint of curiosity.

Without much contemplation, Pranali responded with simplicity, ‘Cappuccino.’

Dr. Sameer, seeking to ensure her comfort, sought further clarification, ‘Nothing more?’

Pranali, replied with a concise ‘No.’

The nearby waiter, attentive to their exchange, approached to take their orders and then quietly retreated to fulfil their requests. A pause enveloped their table, and Pranali, her attention drawn to her fingers, was lost in her thoughts.

Sensing the unusual silence, Dr. Sameer turned his focus towards Pranali. With genuine concern in his eyes, he asked, ‘What’s wrong, Pranali? Do you have anything you want to share with me?’

Pranali, her decision weighing heavily on her, took a deep breath and admitted, ‘Yes.’

Dr. Sameer, his face devoid of emotion, encouraged her to speak her mind, ‘Go ahead.’

With a heavy heart, Pranali voiced her inner turmoil, ‘Actually, I don’t want to marry you.’

Dr. Sameer, taken aback by the unexpected revelation, inquired, ‘What?’

Pranali continued, her voice trembling with sincerity, ‘Sameer, you are genuinely a nice person. If I could, I would marry you. But...’

'Your order, sir,' the waiter interrupted.

Dr. Sameer, maintaining his composure, simply replied, 'Thank you,' and both he and Pranali took their first sips of the cappuccino.

As the coffee provided a brief interlude, Dr. Sameer pressed for an explanation, 'But what?'

Pranali, her eyes drifting out to the street beyond, confessed, 'There is someone I love. And I'm awaiting for his return. Regardless of how long I have to wait, I'll wait for him without a doubt.'

Dr. Sameer, his confusion evident, inquired further, 'Wait? Wait for who?'

Pranali, her gaze still fixed on the road, hesitated momentarily before she revealed the name that held her heart. 'My lover, who is a para commando. MAJOR VIKRANT SHERGIL.'

The revelation seemed to stun Dr. Sameer. He could only reply, 'Ohh.. all right.'

With her attention firmly on the road, Pranali's thoughts began to drift, reminiscing about the past and the feelings that had shaped her.

Dr. Sameer, eager to understand, attempted to draw her back to the present. 'So what happened?

Pranali, her emotions still raw and her story complex, considered her words before speaking, 'It's a long narrative.'

But Dr. Sameer, undeterred and wanting to be a friend even if they couldn't pursue a romantic relationship, gently encouraged her, 'But I'd want to hear it.'

Pranali remained reticent for a moment, then finally conceded, 'All right. I'll let you know. However, let's go outside. The street looks lovely.'

Dr. Sameer, showing his considerate nature, agreed. 'All right, I'll pay the bill and come with you.'

Pranali expressed her gratitude, and as she left the cafe, a cool breeze brushed against her cheeks, imparting a rosy tint to her milk-coloured complexion. She savoured the sensation, closing her eyes briefly to immerse herself in the moment.

Dr. Sameer, after settling the bill, joined her outside. Pranali appreciated the gallant gesture, and the two of them walked together on the charming streets.

As they strolled, Dr. Sameer kindly reiterated his willingness to listen to her story. Pranali, with a gentle smile, agreed, and the stage was set for her to share the intricate tale of her heart and the man she was waiting for.

❑

Contents

Description 5

Author's Note 7

Prologue 9

PART A: Pranali Began the Narration... **15**

CHAPTER 1: The Hearts Embrace 17

CHAPTER 2: Friends for Life 29

CHAPTER 3: Definition of Love 48

CHAPTER 4: My Birthday 59

CHAPTER 5: Siddharth Khanna 76

CHAPTER 6: The Heart's Enchantment 85

CHAPTER 7: Loves Awakening 99

CHAPTER 8: Pranali, Para Commando's Girlfriend 103

PART B: The Narration was Interrupted by Dr. Sameer's Phone Ringtone... 107

CHAPTER 9: I Will Wait for Him 109

CHAPTER 10: Love in the Air 119

CHAPTER 11: The Twist of Fate 126

CHAPTER 12: The Truth Revealed 138

CHAPTER 13: An Eternal Love Story 142

CHAPTER 14: The Fact is, He is a Para Commando 149

CHAPTER 15: Something Worth Waiting For 160

CHAPTER 16: Whispers of Longing 172

CHAPTER 17: The Beckoning of Kashmir 178

CHAPTER 18: Vikrant's Diary 192

CHAPTER 19: The Choice He Made 202

CHAPTER 20: The Biggest Secret Revealed 208

CHAPTER 21: The Haunting Dream 216

CHAPTER 22: A Father's Reluctance 221

CHAPTER 23: Finally, it's Happening 226

CHAPTER 24: Still Waiting 232

CHAPTER 25: Always in My Heart 236

Epilogue 242

❑

Part A

Pranali Began the Narration...

CHAPTER 1

The Hearts Embrace

March 20, 2018, Alsisar, Rajasthan

At last, it's happening. Finally, the wait is over.

I was getting married to my love, my peace and my everything on March 22. Vikrant, the man I adore. The day I met him, everything in my life had altered irrevocably. He is not your typical man. A Para commando, he is. To be honest, I never imagined falling in love with him. I never really imagined becoming a soldier's girlfriend.

Which females have romantic fantasies about men who sleep with TAR-21 rifles as their pillows?

But I loved him. I had the deepest affection for him. And I genuinely believe that I am the luckiest person alive. It wasn't ever intended. It just occurred, or let's call it destiny if you prefer.

Everything occurs for a reason is simply how life tries to tell you through destiny.

The largest family event in India is matrimony. Family members from all generations engage together. Marriage is about the two households as opposed to the two individuals. I've finished explaining now. Let me share my experience with you.

The situation was ideal. Everything was set up. My hands and feet were decorated by mehendi. I had two dozen bangles on each wrist.

All our purchasing was done. I chose to wear a silk sari in navy blue for our marriage while Vikrant decided to wear a white Sherwani.

I started hearing all those typical Bollywood love tunes in my ears. 'Hum tumko nigaho me, bole chudiyaan bole kangana,' and other phrases. Everyone was happy. I was overjoyed. My greatest fantasy was becoming a reality just two days later.

But before we had been married for two days, something unexpected occurred.

I came to the realisation that Vikrant was an Indian soldier after something occurred.

Something made me realise what true suffering is.

Something.....

Vikrant's superiors sent him an email. The border scenario was extremely precarious. So the country required the finest soldier to wear a uniform. So as soon as he read this email, his superior officers told him to return and join his deck. He had to leave. I was astounded to learn all this from Vikrant. For me, it was incredible. I was speechless and unsure of what to say.

Is this actually happening?

I fixed my gaze on Vikrant's irises. They communicated everything he was thinking. His innermost desires were to remain and wed. However, his mind yearned to perform his job. His brain always took precedence over his emotions.

'You are supposed to go, Vikrant. The country requires you,' I said. I don't know how or why I said it, but I did. He widened his eyes at what I said. I believe he anticipated anything but this from me. I grew somewhat nearer to him.

'Yes, Vikrant, you ought to leave. Our wedding can be delayed. But right now, more than anyone else, our country needs you. So you ought to leave. And do not fret. I'll take care of things around here. Just concentrate on your tasks,' I said.

He smiled.

I too.

He gently grasped my face. 'I am very fortunate to have you, Pranali. I love you so much,' he said.

'I love you too.'

We embraced, I had to hold back and control my emotions even though I couldn't. You understand why.

His luggage was full. Leaving everything behind, he then departed. His family, his community, and also me. I was, in fact, very distraught. But I had to restrain my emotions.

When I proposed to him, he told me that being a soldier's wife is not simple.

You understood me correctly. I... proposed... Major Vikrant. Later, I'll relate that story.

But because I adored him, I disregarded all those things. At any cost, I desired my Vikrant.

All he left me with when he went were his recollections. Every second I spent with him in my memory. The day I got introduced to him.....

...

THREE YEARS AGO....

April 2015, Newtown, Kolkata

'Pranali....,' someone yelled my name so loudly and gave me a bear embrace from behind.

I was sitting on a couch working at my desk. On my legs was my laptop. My laptop was crushed. She was Nimrit, my recent two-month housemate. I co-worked with her at the Kolkata based Engineering Company. She is in fact a native of Rajasthan and 18 months before, she entered this company.

She is older than me. As a result, I should technically address her as ma'am, which I did in the beginning. But Nimrit has never been a fan. She used to say that hearing 'mam' from our roommate feels very awkward. So I started addressing her as mam when we were at the office. When we were in the room, I began calling her Nimrit, Nimmi, Nimmu or whatever.

Nimrit is a very decent, compassionate, and kind-hearted lady, to be honest. However, I will never tell her that. She occasionally takes on the roles of my mother, sibling or rival. She was a huge assistance to me when I first started. She assisted me in adjusting to the Bengali way of life. She helped me with my job in the office and is the one who showed me how to live our life. It is known as 'DUNIYADARI.'

'What's going on, and why are you barking?' I angrily inquired, an expression on my face as I sought to understand the cause of her enthusiasm.

She responded, still audibly thrilled but also somewhat exasperated, 'Pranali.'

'Ok. What's up? Why are you shouting my name so loudly?' I asked.

'I got one call.'

I teased her gently by saying, 'From your boyfriend?'

'No. I'm not that fortunate,' she admitted, her energy seemingly draining away in an instant.

'She's really strange. She was like a fire just a moment ago, but now look,' exclaimed my inner voice.

Seeking to understand the situation better, I encouraged her to share the details. 'All right, explain what happened,' I requested.

'I told you about my sibling, do you remember?'

My memory needed a slight jog, so I inquired, 'When?'

She clarified, 'That day.'

Playfully pressing for more details, I questioned, 'Which day was 'that day'?'

'That day,'

I gave up

'What happened, then?' I prodded, my curiosity fully engaged.

'He's coming to Kolkata tonight.'

My response conveyed genuine happiness for her, 'Ah, really?'

She affirmed with enthusiasm, 'Yes. And we're going to meet him tomorrow.' The prospect of this long-awaited reunion seemed to have rekindled her spirits, casting aside the momentary melancholy.

'Okay,' I replied.

'She never told me about her sibling. She does, however, occasionally phone. But I don't know his name, where he resides, what he does, or whether or not he's married,' I thought to myself.

'It's none of your concern; live it. Do your job,' said my inner voice.

I finished my job and went to bed.

…

NEXT DAY

We were scheduled to meet Nimrit's sibling at the evening. I sported blue pants and a pink top. And Nimrit donned a pair of white pants and a blue crepe silk top. The taxi arrived on schedule. However there was a 20 minute delay for the driver. You understand the reason. No? I'll explain.

First and foremost, choosing what to wear was a really difficult job for me. I made the choice to wear a pink short dress last night.

But in the morning, I worried that Nimrit's sibling might not approve. So later, after a long period of thought, I chose to dress in a pink top and blue jeans.

The subsequent phase was makeup. The procedure is step-by-step. I needed to apply gesso first. I then had to put on foundation. Concealer and compact powder follow. I had to use mascara, lipstick, and eyeshadow after that. And with that, I was ready.

Nimrit was ecstatic as usual. She informed me that she would see her sibling in three months. We entered the taxi. Our tardiness cost the cab driver a fee. We didn't want to dispute with him because we were already running behind schedule. We left as soon as the taxi was started by him.

'What's your brother's name, by the way?' I questioned Nimrit.

'Come on Pranali, didn't I tell you that day?'

'Which day?'

'That day,' she said again.

I told myself there was no sense in arguing and asked, 'Can you tell me again, please?'

'Vikrant' she replied.

'What is he doing?' I re-asked.

'He serves in a Para Commando.'

'What ?' I was completely shocked.

'He is a Para Commando, yes. His current posting is in Kolkata, but he had to report himself at Siachin for an assignment before the three months were up. His mission was successfully finished, and he returned yesterday.'

I was genuinely terrified. 'These troops are like monsters,' my father told me. They murder people without any hesitation. I now began to dread Nimrit. This means that for the past two months, I have been living with a lady who is a commando's sister.

'You know what else? He killed 7 terrorists on his most recent assignment.' I never asked the query, but Nimrit provided the response.

She easily said, 'I am very excited to know how many terrorists he killed in this operation.'

We arrived at Victoria Memorial Eastern Garden after 20 minutes. Captain Vikrant was still not there. Near the garden entrance, we were holding out for him. His phone was being dialled by Nimrit. A dark blue Honda Ciaz car suddenly passed us close to the parking area. 'I recognise that vehicle', Nimrit exclaimed with delight.

'How?' I asked surprisingly.

She replied, 'Because... it's my bhaiyya's car.'

'What, do troops even purchase items besides weapons and grenades?' I thought.

Leaving the vehicle, Captain Vikrant emerged. It was for the first time I saw him. His lengthy, never-ending legs were concealed by grey trousers. He wore a light pink coloured formal full sleeves shirt. Just as was anticipated, he had a formal, short haircut. Due to the Indian Army not having any space for Chappris. With his clean-shaven appearance, he was attractive. His left hand held a golden sonata watch, and he sported a pair of black Ray-Ban sunglasses. His shirt was incredibly tight, exposing his ripped physique, broad shoulders, and abs.

He approached us closely. Nimrit said, 'Bhaiyya,' and gave him a tight embrace. He questioned her in a deep, seductive voice, 'How are you, Nimmu?'

'I'm fine, bhaiyya.' She questioned, 'You?'

'My little baby, I'm just fine,' he said.

She pointed at me and said, 'Bhaiyya meet my friend, Pranali.' Captain Vikrant drew near me. I'm not sure why, but my entire body shook. He smelled really nice. My inner voice advised me to ask him what brand of scent he wears.

I responded, 'Shut up.'

He took off his spectacles. His irises are blue, just like the water.

Teri nazrone dil ka kiya jo hashar, asar ye hua..Ohh.. what a beautiful eyes. I just want to drew in it.

'Hello, Pranali,' he greeted.

'Hello, sir.' We exchanged palms. His grip was very harsh. My palm felt as though it were resting on a rock.

He grinned and said, 'I heard a lot about you from Nimmu.'

'What did Nimmi tell him about me?

My hands started to tremble more now.

Captain Vikrant enquired, 'What happened?'

'Aa-huh-no-nothing'

'Are things all right?'

I smiled and said, 'Yes, everything is fine.'

He realised it, shit.

My inner voice told me to act properly.

Into the yard we went. I also noted his figure, which was another aspect of him. Additionally, his trousers were too tight. It was easy to see his firm sexy figure. Will you stop using those expressions, please? What's incorrect with it? The same privileges apply to us women. The bodies of males, like ours, are not particularly interesting to look at. Right ? Men are overly fortunate in that scenario.

What a lovely night it was. The sun was setting, the golden sky. Stars with twinkling lights started to emerge. The breeze was touching our bodies and was extremely cold. Before us, some children were playing. The elderly were having an enjoyable time. Everything there was so serene. Additionally, we received security from none other than Captain Vikrant, a Para Commando.

Nimrit was telling Vikrant everything that had occurred over the previous three months. Even though it was extremely boring,

Vikrant listened to it with great curiosity. He is, of course, his sibling. He was forced to do that. Then Vikrant's time came. He began narrating tales about his work at SIACHIN. Nimrit was now attentively listening to it. However, my fear returned. The tale was finally over.

Nimrit said, 'I'll be back in a minute,' and she walked over to where the kids were playing just in front of us.

I once more heard that seductive voice saying, 'She really likes little children.'

'Aaaaayaa, you're right.' He gave a soft grin.

'By the way, may I ask you a question?' he inquired.

'Of course,' I replied.

'Why were your hands trembling when we shook hands?'

My inner voice muttered, 'Damn, I told you, he noticed it.'

'I've never met a soldier before, you know. And…'

'What ?'

I overheard that.

He repeated his question, this time slightly bit curious, 'Heard what?'

'That... you people are completely heartless, lack empathy, and would kill anyone without hesitation.'

After hearing this, his expression became extremely serious, and then suddenly, a loud 'ha ha ha' erupted from his lips.

I was perplexed. I was curious and inquired, 'What happened?'

'Listen, okay, our troops aren't falling out of the sky. Just like everyone else, we come into this world through the love of our mothers and fathers. We are human beings too, with our own thoughts, feelings, and emotions. But it seems like there are many misconceptions and false rumours about us, and I want to set the record straight.

'First and foremost, we're not emotionless machines. We experience joy, sorrow, fear, and love, just like anyone else. The uniform we wear doesn't make us immune to these emotions. When we are away from our loved ones for long deployments or in challenging situations, it takes a toll on us emotionally.

'In fact, it's often the opposite of what people might think. We hold a deep affection for the people we care about. The bonds we form with our fellow troops are incredibly strong, built on trust and camaraderie forged in some of the most challenging circumstances imaginable. We rely on each other, and that creates a profound sense of brotherhood and sisterhood.

'When we are deployed, we miss our families, friends, and the comforts of home just as much as anyone would. We think about our loved ones constantly, and their support means the world to us. Their letters, emails, and phone calls are like lifelines, keeping us connected to the world outside our duty.

'So, please understand that beneath the uniform and the duty, there's a person with emotions and a heart that cares deeply. We are not distant or unfeeling, but rather, we're driven by a commitment to protect and serve. We're not just soldiers; we're sons and daughters, brothers and sisters, and we value the love and connections we share with our families and friends more than you can imagine.'

I just listened to him and I wanted to hear more. 'Please go ahead,' I said.

He grinned.

'The perception of soldiers as ruthless warriors is a common stereotype, but it's important to clarify that this ruthlessness is directed solely towards those who pose a threat to our nation and its values. Soldiers are not inherently ruthless; they are dedicated individuals who have chosen a path of service, one that prioritizes the protection and well-being of their country.

'Soldiers, like anyone else, lead multifaceted lives. While their primary duty is to defend their nation, they also have personal lives filled with joys, hobbies, and experiences that are no different from those of civilians. Soldiers enjoy life, share moments with loved ones, and partake in activities that bring them happiness.

'Participating in sports is a common interest among soldiers. Sports not only promote physical fitness but also foster camaraderie and teamwork, qualities that are essential in the military. Soldiers compete, train, and celebrate victories, just like any sports enthusiasts.

'However, it is crucial to remember that a soldier's dedication to their country always takes precedence. This commitment is the cornerstone of their profession. They are trained to protect their homeland, uphold its values, and safeguard its citizens, even at the risk of their own lives.

'So, while soldiers may seem tough and disciplined, it is important to understand that their unwavering resolve and the readiness to be ruthless in the face of adversaries is a testament to their dedication and love for their nation. They are protectors, guardians, and patriots who are willing to make sacrifices to ensure the safety and security of their fellow citizens. It is this sense of duty and selflessness that defines the character of an Indian soldier.' His sultry voice affected my heart as much as his words did.

He asked me, 'Tell me about yourself.'

'I'm from Andheri, Mumbai. I received employment at the Engineering Company in Kolkata after completing my computer engineering degree at VJTI in Mumbai. I had to relocate from Mumbai to Kolkata as a result. I've been residing in Newtown for the last two months, sharing a room with Nimrit. For me, Kolkata metropolis was completely new. But Nimrit was very helpful to me in the beginning.'

'Great,' he exclaimed with a grin.

There was a brief stillness.

'Can I have your phone number?' he unexpectedly inquired.

I replied, 'Yes sure. 935905….' and provided him my phone number.

'Thank you. Later, I'll contact you,' he said.

After upsetting the innocent children playing in the yard, Nimrit came back.

'I think, we should leave now,' Vikrant said.

Nimrit responded, 'All right, but let's have dinner together.'

Vikrant retorted, 'Sorry next time, I've got some work to do.'

Nimrit responded with a glum 'Fine.'

Vikrant drove his Ciaz to leave us in our room. He was embraced by Nimrit. I merely shook his hand. He went. He promised to text me, so I was checking my phone every five minutes as a result. And as a result, my office work stayed unfinished.

He still hadn't messaged me at midnight. That person, who? I mean, most females won't give a guy their phone number at first contact. However, I gave him. Therefore, he had a duty to contact me at all costs.

Am I correct? He didn't, though.

'Enough, he won't message you,' my inner voice advised me to get to bed and slumber.

Vikrant's face flashed in front of my eyes as I slept. His charismatic demeanour, his toned figure, his alluring appearance, his blue eyes, his seductive voice, his attractive figure. Excuse me.

❑

CHAPTER 2

Friends for Life

May 2015, Bus Stop, Newtown, Kolkata

'I love you, Pranali. Do you want to be my girlfriend?'

'What in the world are you? How can you propose to a lady you don't even know?'

'Oh, so that is the issue? Then there won't be an issue. I'm Akash, and I've been in love with you for the past two months.'

'What ?'

'Yes. I'm not sure when or how it happened, but it did, and I can't exist without you any longer. Please accept me.'

'Please leave. If not, I'll shatter your teeth and strap them to your feet.'

'You uncivilized lady,' he said.

'How shameless you are? Leave now, or I'll report to the police,' I said.

'I'll leave now, okay? Answer me as soon as you have opportunity. That's all, my love.'

'Do not follow me once more, bastard Akash. I threatened to report you to the authorities if you didn't comply,' I said in mind.

On the bus stop where I was waiting for a bus, the entire episode took place. Nimrit left to the office early because she had some additional work to do.

After I joined my workplace, he started to follow me. He added me as a friend on Instagram as well, but I disregarded it. Actually, he was a chhapri loafer. Why does God create others like him? Completely pointless and a waste of space.

Why do males believe that adding hair accessories like shakalaka boom boom pencils, colouring hair, undoing the top two shirt buttons, riding a KTM, and creating reels can make an impression on a girl? Damn.

I arrived at work. I was in a completely bad mood. I was furious. I sat down and slammed my skull against the desk.

It was my friend and co-worker Shivam Agarwal who said, 'Good morning, Pranali.'

BEFORE 2 MONTHS,

On my first day at the workplace, I was full of happiness. It marked the beginning of my journey towards independence. I dressed in a white formal shirt under a sharp black blazer and matching pants, ready to take on this new chapter. However, Nimrit's sudden illness had led to her absence, leaving me with a bit of uncertainty. She had instructed me to meet Mr. Khanna, who would be my guide on this exciting day.

As I stood at the bus stop, waiting for my ride, my mood took a slight dip when I spotted someone I'd rather not think too highly of - Akash. I had a moment of self-correction, realizing that comparing him to a swine was perhaps unfair to pigs. My apologies to the animals; I should choose my words more carefully. Akash, with his KTM motorcycle, appeared on the scene, and his eyes seemed glued to me. However, I decided to pay him no mind and brushed off his intrusive gaze.

Finally, I arrived at my workplace and entered the lobby. It was abuzz with numerous individuals, each engrossed in their tasks. Nimrit had instructed me to meet Mr. Khanna, but I found myself at a loss when it came to locating his office.

Amidst the crowd, I noticed a man in a sky-blue shirt and black pants, sporting a well-groomed haircut and eyeglasses perched on his nose, well, on his eyes. I made the decision to approach him and seek his assistance.

I said, 'Excuse me,' to him. He swivelled to face me.

'Would you kindly direct me to Mr. Khanna's cabin? Actually, today is my first day,' I said with a grin.

He responded, 'Actually, it's my first day as well, and I'm looking for Mr. Khanna's cabin.'

'Oh, I see,'

I extended my hand and said, 'By the way, my name is Pranali Sharma.' He did not reply. He began contemplating something while looking at my raised palm.

'Hello, I'm Shivam Agarwal. Pleasure to meet you.' We extended palms. His hands began to tremble. This is the issue with people from small towns.

'Me too,' I echoed, grinning slightly.

PRESENT DAY,

'Good morning, I said,' Shivam repeated.

'I'm sorry. I didn't hear.' I responded, 'Good morning.'

'What went on? Is something wrong?' he enquired once more.

'No.. nothing,' I said, lowering my head.

Shivam hailed from a small village in Karnataka. He was your typical boy-next-door, known for his honesty and simplicity.

Shyness was an integral part of his personality. Whenever he tried to strike up a conversation with a girl, his cheeks would flush with embarrassment. I've rarely encountered anyone as genuine as Shivam.

One of his remarkable traits was his diligence. He consistently completed his tasks well ahead of schedule, showcasing his dedication and commitment. Despite his grown-up exterior, Shivam had a childlike innocence about him, and he had a soft spot for his mother, whom he missed dearly.

What truly stood out about Shivam was his unwavering devotion to Lord Shiva. Before embarking on any endeavour, he would offer his prayers to the deity, seeking blessings and guidance. It was this spiritual connection that added depth to his character, reflecting his faith and values.

'Good Morning guys', he was Pratik Verma.

BEFORE 2 MONTHS

Shivam and I looked for someone who could assist us. But speaking to strangers who are dressed in casual attire can be extremely uncomfortable. Shivam exhibited complete introversion in it. I had to move forward as a result.

'Is this your first day?' asked a person coming we from behind us. We turned to gaze at the person.

He introduced himself as 'Pratik Verma.'

'Ha.. he. Hello, I'm Pranali Sharma' and 'I'm Shivam Agarwal.'

'Is it your first day?' he inquired once more. He continued, 'Because I've never seen you here before.'

'It is our first day, yes. Actually, we are searching for Mr. Khanna's quarters. So, would you kindly assist us?' I asked.

'You'd better follow me,'

'Thank you, God,' I thought.

We began to pursue him. With his trademark pervy smile he said, ‘By the way, your voice is so sweet.’ I found it a little uncomfortable. ‘Like you,’ he continued.

‘Oh, thank you,’ I exclaimed with a grin.

Shivam, a recluse, was on my side, and Pratik, a pervert, was on the other.

PRESENT DAY,

Shivam greeted Pratik by saying, ‘Good morning.’

Pratik said, ‘My good morning wish was also for you.’

‘Yes, good morning,’ I mumbled while feigning a grin. Once more, my cranium hit the table. Both Shivam and Pratik were confused.

Pratik, in our company, was quite the character – a slightly mischievous, fun-loving person. His main focus always seemed to be on having a good time and looking stylish. However, his Achilles’ heel was undoubtedly girls. He had a tendency to be easily swayed and fooled when it came to them. It was almost as it his main goal in life was to flirt with any girl nearby.

You know the type, right? The guy who’s never really serious and is always striving to be the cool one in the group. To be honest, whenever he tried to pull off this act, it often came across as a bit foolish. Annoying, isn’t it?

BEFORE 2 MONTHS

Shivam and I were directed by Pratik to Mr. Khanna’s stateroom. We made our way to the house.

‘Listen, Mr. Khanna is an extremely rigid person. You should behave properly at all times. Avoid using a loud voice. Never say more or less. Best wishes. If you live, we’ll cross paths once more.’ My heartbeat picked up after hearing Pratik say these things. My hands and thighs began to tremble. You are now wondering what Shivam must have experienced, right?

I greeted Mr. Khanna according to protocol and asked, 'May I come in, sir?'

'Yes, please come in,'

Shivam and I walked into Mr. Khanna's office, and from the moment we met him, he exuded confidence while maintaining a humble demeanour. His warm grin and kind eyes immediately put us at ease. Mr. Khanna's side-combed salt and pepper hair was impeccably styled, giving him a distinguished look. Despite his age, he carried himself with professionalism and experience that commanded respect. His glossy black leather shoes and perfectly tailored suit, complete with a pocket square, reflected his attention to detail.

As we spoke to him, it was evident that Mr. Khanna had lived a full life, one that had seen both joy and challenges. His facial wrinkles hinted at the stories he could tell, and being around him made everyone feel more confident, thanks to his calming presence and quiet strength. He gave the impression of being an intelligent, well-informed, and highly trustworthy individual.

We introduced ourselves to Mr. Khanna and handed over our papers, but Shivam continued to tremble with nerves. After a quick review of our files, Mr. Khanna picked up the office phone and made a call, instructing someone to come to his cabin. He then resumed reading or organizing his paperwork.

My ears were still ringing from Pratik's words earlier, but to be entirely honest, Mr. Khanna didn't come across as rigid or imposing as Pratik had made him out to be. After a brief wait, a woman entered the cabin, marking the next chapter in this intriguing encounter.

She asked without even recognizing our presence, 'You called me sir?'

'Yes.' Mr. Khanna introduced us to Sonal as Shivam Agarwal and Pranali Sharma, respectively.

'She is Sonal Malhotra, Pranali and Shivam.'

'Hello,' I greeted Sonal.

That shy creature said, 'Ha.. hello,' adjusting his glasses.

'It is nice to meet you,' Sonal said.

'They are the newest members of team 7, Sonal,' said Mr. Khanna.

'Team 7?' I questioned in my head.

Mr. Khanna instructed Sonal, 'Tell them then how our company operates and what their roles are in this company.'

Sonal nodded.

'Follow me,' she said to us. I and Shivam and I followed her.

'Ma'am,' I inquired as eagerly as I could, 'What is team 7?'

'I'll describe it to you,' she responded, 'Follow me.' She led the way to the gathering space. She urged everyone to take a seat.

'Thank you.'

As the projector lit up the screen, a PPT presentation came to life. The presenter, a woman with a calm demeanour, embarked on a journey through the company's history, its current objectives, and the ambitious long-term plans. To be honest, it was, well, pretty dull. The graphs, charts, and statistics seemed to soar to heights beyond my comprehension.

Yet, in the midst of this rather tedious presentation, one person stood out. Shivam, sitting beside me, leaned in with a focused gaze. He seemed to hang on to every word, his attention undivided by the droning monotony of the slides. It was as if he saw something in that presentation that I couldn't quite grasp.

In the realm of business presentations, where figures and forecasts can easily overwhelm, Shivam's unwavering attention was a testament to his dedication and perhaps his ability to find meaning in even the driest topics.

After what appeared to be a tedious lesson, she questioned us, 'Understood?'

'Yes, ma'am,' Shivam yelled in response

'But Ma'am, what is Team 7?' I questioned.

'Look, we work on projects in teams at this firm. As a result, the job is finished quickly and new, creative ideas are continued. There are 5 people on each squad. You both belong to our squad, which is group 7.'

'So, who are the other two squad members?'

'Nimrit Shergil and Pratik Verma.'

I was overjoyed to be on my roommate Nimrit's squad.

PRESENT DAY,

'Listen Pranali, I think we are close friends, in order to share everything with us. There's no need to be uncomfortable,' Sonal said.

She was like the Barbie doll of our group, always impeccably dressed with a remarkable fashion sense. Her attention to detail was astonishing – she would even change her nail polish daily to match her outfit.

This gifted young woman shared a temperament much like Nimrit's – kind-hearted and warm-hearted. There was something else about her that I couldn't help but notice. Whenever Pratik, one of our friends, tried to flirt with other girls, she seemed uncomfortable with it. It was clear that she had strong feelings for Pratik.

As time elapsed, I would come to understand the reason behind her feelings.

As a result, Sonal was the Barbie girl of our group, Pratik was the cool man and pervert, and Shivam was the baby boy and introvert. Squad 7 was regarded as the best squad overall because of this. We used to finish tasks ahead of schedule. We had a mutual agreement and went beyond being a team. We resembled a family. Father Shivam, mother Nimrit, younger boy Pratik, his girlfriend Sonal, and older daughter Pranali made up the family.

Pratik's trademark grating chuckle accompanied his question, 'Did you have a breakup?'

'Will you just shut up?' Sonal commanded.

I told them everything that had occurred that morning as I was leaving for work.

Pratik growled once more, 'Ohh.. so that's the issue.'

'Pranali, don't think about it.' Sonal attempted to imitate my mother by saying, 'The more you think about it, the more depressed you will feel.'

'You are correct; you should pay attention to mother Sonal.' It was Pratik once more.

God of annoyance.

'Stop talking,' Sonal retorted. She continued, 'You all boys are the same.'

Shivam and Pratik gave her disturbed glances. I believe Pratik received it correctly.

'What's wrong with it,' she questioned.

'Oh really?' Pratik questioned.

'Yes, truly,' Sonal retorted.

'I am unique.'

'From what direction?

'Every,' Pratik answered.

'Why do you then always look at Arti?' she questioned. Shivam, Sonal, Pratik and I all turned to face Arti, who was seated right behind Pratik. In our workplace, she was the cutest girl. How then could Pratik, who is perverse, miss the opportunity?

'I never do it,' he said.

'You do,' she said.

'Be quiet,'

'You must be quiet.' And as usual, their pointless argument began. Shivam and I were having fun.

Shivam called me, 'Pranali. Do you feel good right now?'

'Yes,' I replied.

'Just put the morning's events in the past.'

I responded, 'Okay,' with a sincere grin on my face.

Stop, you two, why are you fighting, Nimrit yelled as she entered the group.

Sonal remarked, 'This idiot initiated this fight.'

Pratik argued, 'No, this fight was initiated by this pig's daughter.'

'All right, go return to your work,' Nimrit commanded.

We went to a café after finishing our job in the office. Shivam provided the delight. We then went back to our apartment.

I didn't even eat supper that night because I was so exhausted. I only dressed and lay on the bed. However, I continued to monitor my WhatsApp to see if Vikrant had messaged me or not. He didn't. It had been three days since that day. He hasn't messaged me yet, though.

Come on, yaar, how is this even possible? Is he acting this way on purpose or is he actually busy? I asked myself, 'Is he trying to show me attitude?'

Then I made the decision to question Nimrit about Vikrant. I then decided to abandon my goal. Nothing else was an option; I could only wait.

...

Finally, the weekend had arrived, and Sunday was bathed in brilliant sunshine. The warm breeze enveloped everything, creating a sense of tranquillity. Yet, there was something that kept coming up, Nimrit's voice, a constant ache in my heart. I couldn't help but be grateful for the air conditioning that seemed to save me from drowning in my own thoughts.

In reality, Sunday is a precious gift for those who toil tirelessly throughout the week. It's the one day when people can engage in their favourite activities and cherish quality moments with their families. The anticipation of Sunday is akin to how peacocks yearn for rain; it's filled with hope and excitement.

But here's the twist - the true joy of Sunday often finds its way into Saturday. Do you ever feel like the entire Sunday is spent dreading the arrival of Monday? It's like a shadow that looms over the day, reminding us of the impending workweek.

Sunday, a day of rest and leisure, can sometimes be bittersweet, as the impending Monday casts its long shadow. So, while we long for the relaxation and happiness Sunday promises, we can't help but feel the ever-approaching Monday lurking just around the corner.

At 10am, I awoke. Actually, we had a modest party last night. Our celebration was on Saturday night. On that night, we would perform dances, sing songs, view movies, and more. We lay in bed at 1am in the morning.

I was reading the book 'I will go with you,' which had that as its title.

She was Nimrit, who shouted 'Pranali.'

'Actually,' she admitted, 'I have a meat craving today.'

'Of pig?' I playfully questioned.

'Pranali,' she muttered.

'Sorry. What do you need from me, then?'

If I was going to listen to her quickly, she said, 'I want you to make biryani for me.' I grinned. She believed that by looking like that, she had persuaded me.

'Forget,' I replied.

'Come on, Pranali,'

'No.'

'I am your senior, so listen. So please do as I say, okay' she said, attempting to sound intelligent.

'Excise me. You are my senior in the workplace. We are both the same here,' I said.

'Come on, Pranali, yaar.' She pleaded for help with a fake innocent expression on her face.

'Okay, I'll get there just because you said so.'

'Liar, say na, you too have a craving for biryani,' a voice inside me said.

She hugged me and said, 'Thank you, thank you, thank you.'

I said, holding up a novel to her, 'Aa ok, but I will make it tonight, not now, I want to finish this novel.'

'Okay,' she retorted.

After a few moments of silence, Nimrit questioned, 'You know something?'

'What now?'

She remarked, 'Vikkie bhaiyya loves biryani so much.'

'Now who is Vikkie?' I questioned.

'Vikrant bhaiyya, occasionally I refer to him as Vikkie. Everyone in our village used to nickname him Vikkie,' she said.

'Pranali, this is your opportunity,' my inner voice said.

'Why don't we call him to our biryani party tonight,' I asked Nimrit.

'Idea is fantastic,' she retorted.

She jokingly remarked, 'Finally you started using your brain.' I looked at her angrily.

She continued, 'But what if he's busy tonight?'

I said, 'First, at the very least, call him. Then, we'll see if he shows up or not.'

She said, 'Okay,' and went out onto the terrace to make a call.

'But why are you so eager to meet Captain Vikrant, Pranali?' my inner voice questioned.

I retorted, 'No, no, nothing like that.'

'Really'

'Yes its 7 days up and he didn't messages me. That's why….'

'Ok ok..'

'Stay quiet, let me complete this novel', I said to myself.

'But I hope he will come tonight', I said in my mind.

'Got you,' exclaimed my inner voice.

'Shut up'.

After few minutes, Nimrit returned. Her face was bright. It said, Vikrant is coming tonight.

'Bhaiyya is coming tonight', she said.

'Yes yes yes..', I said in my mind.

'Oh really', I said acting like.. its okay then.

'Yes'

'All right', I said with smile on my face.

I had already planned what I would do and say to Captain Vikrant. He will first sound the bell. I will then proceed to unlock the door. Then I will respond 'Welcome, sir' with complete confidence. He will then enter.

Then, I will say, 'Please have a seat,' and I will say it with complete assurance. He will then respond, 'Yes, thank you.' We will then engage in discussion. Then, when it is appropriate, I will ask Captain Vikrant if he has my phone number. He will then respond 'Yes.'

Then I'll ask 'Why haven't you messaged me yet?' He will then acknowledge his error and apologise to me. And I will pardon him with all my heart.

Give me your number and I'll massage you, I'll add after that. I'll send him a WhatsApp message as a concluding step.

'You make me proud, Pranali. What a wise decision you made. Finally, you are an adult,' I told myself.

'Rubbish one,' replied my inner voice.

It was 7pm Vikrant will arrive at any time, according to Nimrit's announcement. I last noticed myself in the reflection. I wore a blue outfit. I put on pink lipstick and showered in my best scent. Bell finally ranged. Their pulse quickened as their bell ranged. 'Do everything as it is intended,' I told myself. I moved forward towards the entrance very slowly while retaining all of my self-confidence. However, Nimrit unexpectedly moved forward and unlocked the door.

A first step successfully failed.

He was greeted by Nimrit. He wore a full-sleeved black blouse with black bottoms. the same bright blue eyes.

'Ankhon me teri, ajab si ajab si adaye hain', my inner voice said.

Only one distinction stood out to me about him. And that was his last time shaving clean. His scant whiskers, however, were now visible. potentially a length of 4 millimetres. And let me tell you, he had a very seductive appearance. Nothing else was altered. The same lean frame, wide shoulders, firm figure… excuse me.

Every single word I intended to say was said by her.

Step two was unsuccessful too.

Vikrant approached me. He smelled nice, just like the previous time.

'Please,' my inner voice begged, 'Ask him what perfume he wears this time.'

'Have you lost your mind?'

'Please'

'Shut up,' I commanded myself.

'Hello, Pranali,' said Vikrant, extending his right palm.

'Hello, sir,' I said as I shook hands. My hands trembled once again. He observed once more.

'Go to hell, Pranali Sharma,' said my inner voice.

I said, 'Please have a seat,' with all the assurance I could muster.

Yes, the final step worked.

During our gathering, Vikrant, Nimrit, and I engaged in a delightful conversation, reminiscing about our childhood memories. Vikrant and Nimrit, in particular, couldn't help but recall one unforgettable incident from their early days.

'You know, Pranali,' Vikrant began with a smile, 'We had this neighbour, an aunt who was quite stern and strict. She had a cat, and oddly enough, the cat seemed to inherit her sternness. Back then, we used to play cricket, and on one particular day, I was in top form. I hit a magnificent six, and, well, it happened to land right on her cat.'

A chorus of laughter erupted as we imagined the comical scene of a cricket ball making a rather unexpected target out of the neighbour's feline companion. Vikrant, despite his usually composed demeanour, blushed ever so slightly, feeling somewhat self-conscious about the memory.

'That aunty,' Nimrit chimed in after sharing a hearty laugh, 'She was quite upset about it. She complained to our family and didn't hold back in her criticisms of Vikkie Bhaiyya here.'

Vikrant's cheeks turned even rosier as we chuckled at the memory. His protective instincts for his younger self clearly hadn't waned over the years.

'And you know what Vikkie Bhaiyya did that evening' Nimrit continued, her eyes twinkling with mischief. 'He decided to teach her a lesson, and, well, let's just say her house ended up with a many broken window panes that day.'

Another round of laughter filled the room as we pictured the determined young Vikrant venting his frustration in such a memorable way.

Amidst the jovial atmosphere, Nimrit excused herself to check on the status of the biryani in the kitchen, leaving Vikrant, Pranali, and their shared childhood memories to warm the room with laughter and nostalgia.

'Pranali, this is it; this is your chance.' My inner voice told me to ask him why he hadn't messaged me yet, so I collected all of my chakra and energy and said, 'Nice shirt.'

'Idiot.'

'Oh, thanks,' Vikrant said.

After a few moments of silence, I inquired, 'Can I ask you something?'

'Yes off course,'

I asked, 'Why didn't you... message me?'

'Oh, I'm sorry,' he said, 'You know, I was a little busy last week.'

'What do you mean by busy?' I asked in my head.

'After that day, we actually had a meeting where it was agreed that I would travel to Bengaluru to meet with our Commanding Officer to discuss some important matters. After coming back, I had to shift to HQ Recruiting Zone at Bhowanipore from HQ near Fort William. I really forget to message you during all of this,' he confessed.

'It's okay,' I retorted.

He said, 'I'll message you tonight.'

'No need,' Oh, I did say it. I'm not sure where my assurance to state that came from.

I made it plain, 'Because.. give me your mobile number, and I will message you.'

'Oh, All right,' he sighed in relief and said, 'Take 992234.....'

And was saved.

Biryani had been prepared, and we gathered around the dining table. I served Vikrant a steaming plate of biryani, and the fragrant aroma filled the room. But something unexpected happened when Vikrant took his first bite – he closed his eyes in sheer delight. I exchanged a puzzled glance with Nimrit, who had a satisfied grin on her face.

Without hesitation, Vikrant declared, 'Mind-blowing.' Nimrit burst into laughter, and I couldn't help but feel a sense of accomplishment. 'This is the best biryani I've ever had,' Vikrant continued, his appreciation shining through. 'You know, when I'm on my missions, there's only one thing I truly miss, and that's this delicious food variety. I'm so grateful, Pranali.'

His usual composure seemed to vanish as he happily devoured the biryani, resembling a child lost in the joy of a favourite treat. It was an adorable sight that warmed my heart.

After our satisfying meal, Vikrant suggested, 'I would really appreciate some ice cream now.' Nimrit enthusiastically agreed, and we decided to head to "Happiness Ice Cream." The nightlife in Kolkata was vibrant, with a pleasant and brisk temperature. The stars sparkled above us, and the moon added to the enchanting atmosphere. Vikrant took the wheel, with Nimrit joining me in the car.

As we sped through the city, Vikrant expertly manoeuvred the car, maintaining a perfect balance of speed and safety. We couldn't help but enjoy the thrill of the ride. Finally, we arrived at "Happiness Ice Cream," where a digital screen displayed a tempting array of flavours. It was a tough decision – which flavour should I choose?

The evening was filled with simple pleasures – delicious food, fast rides through the city, and the excitement of choosing the perfect ice cream flavour. It was a moment of pure happiness, and I couldn't help but savour every second of it with Vikrant and Nimrit by my side.

'Which flavour do you like?' Vikrant questioned.

'Butterscotch,' I said in response. Vikrant smiled.

'And you, Nimmu?'

'I'll take vanilla.' He then requested '2 butterscotch and 1 vanilla.' Even Vikrant enjoyed the taste of butterscotch.

'Am.. it's good,' I said.

'Do you enjoy it?' Vikrant questioned.

'So much,' I answered. Ice cream consumed, it was time to head back home.

Nimrit said, 'Bhaiyya, I'll drive the car.'

'Is she even capable of operating a vehicle? Does She have a licence?' I asked myself.

Giving her the key, Vikrant said, 'Okay.' Nimrit was behind the wheel. I felt slightly apprehensive. Vikrant joined me by occupying the rear. We arrived in our chamber without incident. Vikrant wished us farewell before departing. He had to travel 19km to reach Bhowanipore.

My inner voice advised me to message him. But what to?;That's the question.

I typed a note after spending an hour in deep thought. When you find out which letter I wrote, you'll be surprised.

"Itz Pranali" yes, it was the note, which was sent.

After some time, he responded.

'Hello, reached?'

'Yes,' I said, 'Just a moment ago.'

What should I say next? I began to consider.

'You looked so beautiful today', he messaged. It was totally surprising for me. 'Thank you sir,' I replied.

'Hey don't call me sir. Just call me Vikrant. After all, we are now friends, right?'

'Yes sir,' I replied. 'I mean Vikrant,' I corrected.

'You cook really well Pranali'.

'Thank you so much,' I replied with smile emoticon.

'By the way, what are your hobbies?' he asked an unexpected question. Now how does one reply?

'I like to listen old songs, watch movies and read novels'

'Great,' he replied. Now their was nothing great in it.

'Yours ?' I asked.

'Reading novels, watching anime and cartoons, playing badminton and cricket, etc.'

'Watching cartoons?'

'Yes, my favourite cartoons are Doremon and Shinchan,' he retorted with a smile emoticon, 'And Naruto is my favourite anime. Actually, I have a very busy agenda every day, but I still find time for the things I enjoy,' he continued. Our discussion was going really well. We exchanged preferences and dislikes with one another.

His preferences-

Hero- Shah Rukh Khan

Heroine- Deepika Padukone

Movie- Mohabattein

Song- Hum tumko nigaho me

Colour- Black and blue

Food- Chicken biryani (specially made by me)

Sweet- Ras malai

I will spare you the rest of our discussion.

It marked the start of both my happy times and our new relationship.

#thankyouwhatsapp

❑

CHAPTER 3

Definition of Love

June 2015, Newtown, Kolkata

Life was going well for me. I had come to enjoy my job at the office, and things were going smoothly. My close friend Nimrit and I were having a marvellous time as always. But there was a new addition to my life – a Para Commando friend named Vikrant.

We started talking quite frequently, usually setting our conversation time for 10 to 11 pm Each conversation left me pleasantly surprised and excited. We even made it a tradition to meet up every Sunday to catch up on the events of the past week.

Vikrant was a busy person with a packed schedule, but he always managed to find time for his family and friends, including me. It was always a joy to spend time with him.

One day at the office, things took an interesting turn. When Nimrit and I arrived, our colleagues Shivam and Sonal were already hard at work. We exchanged morning greetings, but something seemed off with Sonal. She looked furious, and her eyes were practically on fire as she pounded the keyboard keys aggressively. Her face was flushed red, and it was clear that something was bothered her. One person was notably absent that day – our colleague Pratik.

I took a seat and asked Sonal, 'By the way, where is Pratik?' She remained silent. I was instructed to gaze to my right by Shivam. I twisted. That idiot was busy making out with a new employee in our workplace.

'Oh, so that's why Sonal is so irate today,' I guessed. Pratik had to pay for it, I was aware of that. Sonal won't abandon him. Sonal was already very enraged when Pratik did something that fanned the flames even further. He continued to put his palm on the newcomer's shoulder. By the way, her name is Divya.

Sonal declared, 'That's enough,' and stood up. She marched enraged in the direction of Pratik. As Sonal approached him, Pratik abruptly withdrew his hand from Divya's shoulder. 'Pratik is going to die,' Nimrit declared.

We didn't hear anything Sonal said to Pratik or Divya. She took hold of his hand and led him over to team 7's desk. 'What's wrong with you Sonal?', Pratik asked.

'What's wrong with me, you ask? How are you doing, Pratik? Why can't you restrain yourself?' Sonal asked angrily, 'Is it necessary to flirt with every girl you meet' The atmosphere was strained. We had the impression that there would be a major spectacle. Nimrit and Shivam silently examined them. Their disagreement involved maturing. Pratik was making an effort to fight back, but Sonal was in the driver's seat.

Finally, Sonal yelled, 'Leave Pratik, you will never understand my feelings,' and she ran towards the balcony area while sobbing. Yes, she was crying as she made that statement. I felt stunned, because she has never before been seen weeping. Nimrit called Pratik a 'duffer' and followed Sonal to the balcony. Pratik was bewildered.

'What happened', Pratik inquired. It was now my time. I commanded him to follow me and led him to a part of the foyer where there was less of a crowd. Shivam also came after us.

'Do you have any common sense?' I questioned Pratik with concern.

'What occurred?' he seemed puzzled.

I asked, 'Don't you see tears in her eyes?'

He admitted, 'I noticed, but for what purpose?'

'Seriously?' I couldn't believe it.

'What?' he remained perplexed.

'Are you oblivious, she loves you. Don't you understand such a simple thing?'

'What? Really?'

I affirmed, 'Yes.'

'I never knew it,' he confessed.

I couldn't help but express my frustration, 'Because you are an idiot. And right now, you will talk to Sonal. Make her smile.'

He was uncertain, 'Who, me?'

'No, your ghost, you fool,' I couldn't resist a sarcastic reply.

'All right, I'll do that,' he replied.

I, Pratik and Shivam, we three went to the balcony where Nimrit and Sonal were already there. As I pushed Pratik towards Sonal, I beckoned Nimrit our way. To offer them privacy, we only stood there while partially closing the balcony door. We wished to know what would happen, after all.

Softly, Pratik said, 'Sona.' Sonal remained silent. Once more, he hailed her, 'Oye Sona.'

'What?' she angrily retorted.

Pratik questioned 'Sona, what happened, why are you crying?' Sonal swung around to face Pratik.

She again retorted rudely, 'Because I love it, that's why.' From behind the door, we chuckled.

'Can I share something with you?'

'What would you like to inform me? How wonderful is your new friend? How stunning is she?'

'No, you already know it,' the idiot said, adding more gasoline to the blaze.

'I just wanted to let you know that.'

'What?'

'That I love.' Sonal questioned startlingly,

'What?' like Sonal , we too were taken aback. I never imagined Pratik would have the courage to tell Sonal that.

'I love you, that's true. But I never said it because, well, I always felt like I wouldn't measure up to you. You're such an accomplished and diligent woman, good at everything, like Miss Perfection. Now, let's take a look at me. I do my job because I have to, no big dreams, no seriousness about life. In simple terms, you can call me a "bade baap ki bigdi aulad."

'So, I kept all my feelings for you hidden deep inside my heart because of this. And there's one more thing, though you might not believe it. When I first laid eyes on you, I fell in love. But, that's about it.'

We were surprised because we had no idea Pratik could talk in a way that made sense. Sonal approached Pratik cautiously. Both of her palms remained on his shoulder. Pratik grinned.

Nimrit exclaimed with enthusiasm, 'Kiss him.' Shivam gave her a startled and peculiar-looking look as he gazed.

As Sonal drew even closer to Pratik, imagine what happened? Sonal kicked the most tender and painful area of Pratik's body. Sonal kicked Pratik's testicles, to be exact.

Pratik yelled, 'Aaaaa...'

We liked it, but Sonal felt bad.

Shivam also cried out in agony.

'Where you kicked jaaneman? At least, you should have considered our babies.'

'Pratik, I'm so sorry. I had no intention of doing it. Does it hurt?' Sonal questioned Pratik.

She received a very odd and amusing glance from Pratik.

'Who told you that? No, no, of course not. Actually, I liked it. I really liked it.' He again made a comedic face and said, 'Look how happy I am after having my balls crushed by you.'

'Okay'.

'What's up, you idiot?' He cried out, 'Don't you see my condition,' as if it was a baby.

'Wait, I'll help you,'

'No, no, this…. after we got married. Please control your feelings.'

'Idiot, extend your palm to me.' Sonal said, 'I'll help you stand up.'

'Oh, okay,' said Pratik. Sonal assisted him in standing. They exchanged glances for a moment before starting to smile—no, laugh. They gave each other hugs. Nimrit embraced me. 'Yes,' Shivam replied.

We were still curious as to what would occur next. So we were the only ones there. From behind, someone suddenly taped my arm. I mistook her for Nimrit. 'Wait no,' I commanded. I felt a touch on my shoulder from behind once more. I turned around and irritably asked, 'What yaar?' It was, indeed, Mr. Khanna's palm. He was in front of us. He appeared enraged.

'What are you three doing in this place?' he inquired, 'Are you spying on something?'

Nimrit responded, 'Nothing, sir.' To see what was happening on the balcony, he cautiously opened the door. Oh, dear. We believed that Mr. Khanna would not permit this in his workplace.

However, out of the blue, he gently grinned and said, ‘So finally.’ I suppose he hoped to see them all together as well.

‘He isn’t really that obnoxious,’ my inner voice said.

‘You three, have you ever heard the term ‘privacy’ pronounced?’

‘Yes, sir,’ we shamelessly replied.

‘You are aware of the definition of that word?’ he inquired once more.

Once more, we shamelessly respond, ‘Yes sir.’

‘Oh, that was really, really excellent.’

We broke all standards for shamelessness when we uttered the words ‘thank you, sir.’

‘Go back and finish your work now.’ We went back to the place of work. After a while, Sonal and Pratik also came back. Now they were ecstatic. Nimrit departed for submitting some documents to Mr. Khanna.

Shivam went by the name ‘Pranali.’

‘Yes’

‘Can I ask you a question?’

‘Of course,’

‘Something of.... Nimrit?’ he exclaimed, surprised and delighted.

‘What information about Nimrit did he want to seek out?’ I said in mind.

‘Yes sure, ask’.

‘Does Nimrit have a boyfriend?’

‘What?’ There was a burst of laughter coming from my lips as I said, ‘Ha ha ha.’ I disturbed everyone. Everyone shushed me as they turned to face me. I said, ‘Sorry,’ to everyone.

‘Tell me, does she have a partner,’ he softly enquired again.

'She doesn't have a partner, so no.'

He questioned, 'Seriously?' with a wise expression.

'Yes, but why do you ask me all this?' I excitedly questioned.

'Because.... Since I love her.'

'What? Ha ha ha,' another fit of laughter erupted from my lips. I irritated everyone once more. Once more, everyone silenced me. And I apologised once more.

'Are you serious?', I asked him. mainly because it was absurd. In other words, I knew Shivam felt something for Nimrit, but I never imagined it would be this.

'Yes, I love her dearly.'

'Do you know something, though?'

'What?'

Her sibling is a member of the 'Para Special Force.'

'What?' This time it was Shivam who startled everyone, not me.

Sonal questioned, 'What's wrong with you guys?'

'No nothing,' I apologised.

His eyes clearly displayed his dread. His lips were closed tight. He appeared to be very naive. 'Don't worry, I'll assist you,' I assured him while grinning.

'Thank you,' he said, his visage displaying both fear and a smile. Two members of 'Team 7' made their affection known on that day. But the real issue was whether Nimrit truly loved Shivam. And if she is certain, will Vikrant approve of their love marriage? Nimrit and I came back to our room from the workplace. Whether Nimrit loves Shivam back or not was the one question that kept coming up in my head. I had to locate it. I then took on the task.

As usual, we began chatting about silly inconsequential topics after dinner. Even though I now consider those topics to be nonsense, at the time, they seemed more significant than anything else in the universe. I made the decision to find out Nimrit's opinion of Shivam.

'What do you think of Pratik, Nimrit?'

'Pratik? Although he occasionally acts foolishly, he is generally decent.'

'And Sonal?'

'She is a contemporary diva, kind-hearted, and model-like,'

'Shivam,' I asked. She hesitated before saying, 'Aa.' I'm not sure why. Then she added, 'He's a really nice person. A true gentleman,'

'And?'

'And he is charming too,'

'Really?' She blushed as she said, 'Yes.'

'Hey, why did your face turn red?' I made fun of her.

'Anything Prana,'

I said, 'You know what, I think he likes you.'

'What?' she exclaimed startlingly. 'Did he say anything to you?' she questioned.

I responded, 'No no, not at all.'

'So don't say foolish things,' she said. 'Why would he care about me? He is younger than I am.'

'But when you genuinely love someone, age doesn't matter.'

'He is also very introverted'.

'So tell me something straight. What if he were to ask you out?'

She replied with a sweet smile, 'Um... To be honest, I don't have any reason to refuse him.'

'Really?'

I'm not sure, but I believe she attempted to hide her feelings when she said, 'I feel fast asleep, I'm going.' She obviously still loves Shivam, as was now evident. The only remaining query concerned Vikrant. How will he react to it?

'Hello Prana, what are you doing', It was message from Mr. Men in Olive Green, Captain Vikrant Shergil.

'He will survive for 100 years,' I told myself.

'Just relaxing. You?' I typed.

'Same.'

'Yes. Do you know what happened in my workplace today?'

'You know, I'm not the Himalayan Tapasvi, and I still haven't attained enlightenment. Therefore, regrettably, I am unsure of what happened at your workplace today.'

'Very funny,' I retorted.

'Thank you,'

'Listen, Vikrant,'

'Ok. Call me.'

'Ok'. I called his cell phone number. His caller song ran.

He answered a call.

'Go ahead,' and I proceeded to narrate the entire tale of Pratik and Sonal. He was listening it, I mean reading it very eagerly. 'How did you know?,' you ask? because he responded quickly and used that particular emoticon. He was overjoyed for them both. The narration is done.

I said, 'I have a question I want to ask you.'

'Go ahead'

'What do you think of love, Vikrant?'

'Well, to be honest, I never gave it any consideration. However, while truly loving someone is not wrong, being fulfilled is more crucial. In the universe, there are two types of couples. First, someone who enters a relationship solely for sexual fulfilment. Their bond is like raindrops dropping. It initially feels nice, but as time goes on, it gradually begins to feel gloomy and ugly. As a consequence, this relationship is kept up for a short while. Then, as the divisions widen, the relationship ends.

'They truly love each other, which is the second type of relationship. They have a pickle-like relationship. As time passes, it gets tastier. Here, disagreements might also occur. But they manage it because they have mutual confidence. As a result, the relationship is eternal. As a result, we should truly adore, respect, and care for our partner. We have no right to love anyone if we are incapable of doing it. Believe that.'

Following its hearing, I was in awe. Literally every single phrase touched my heart. I never imagined that any man could hold these opinions. Wasn't every word he spoke heartfelt and true?

I re-asked, 'What do you think about love marriage?'

'It's not about affection or planning, you see. Does your companion really deserve your trust? Do you truly adore your partner? Will he or she look after you for the rest of your life? If the response is 'yes,' you may continue.'

My inner voice warned, 'This man is going to kill you with his words.'

Then, with all my confidence, I inquired, 'Will you allow Nimrit to have a love marriage if she so chooses?' Such bravery on my part. He did not reply. He hung up on the conversation. I assumed he was enraged. After waited for thirty minutes. He didn't contact or message me.

I got a call.

Vikrant's was it.

'Mummy's call, I'm sorry.'

I retorted, 'No problem.'

'Look, it is entirely up to her to choose whom she will love or wed. Yet as you are aware, I am her older sibling. My main duty is to secure her future. Therefore, I will undoubtedly put that individual to the test; if he truly cares about my sister, he can become my beloved 'Jijaji.'

'What a loving and caring brother he is. God ought to have given me a sibling like him.' I argued in my head, 'I mean, like him, not him.'

❑

CHAPTER 4
My Birthday

July 22, 2015, Newtown, Kolkata

I was born 23 years ago on July 22, 1994. I turned a certain age. Everybody should keep in mind that their birthday is a very significant day of the year. Because on this day, you become a very significant individual in the lives of others. It is the kind of day when people naturally start acceptably nice around you. So, savour each moment of the day. Because the same people will not handle you the same way tomorrow. And it represents one of society's hard realities.

Off course, since Nimrit was my roommate, she was the first to congratulate me. My parents remained up till the early hours of the morning to wish me. I was very happy after their call, but I also felt bad for them because they had to sacrifice their much-loved sleep in order to wish their daughter, who actually never recalls their birthdates.

I received calls from all of my close acquaintances. When the phone calls finally ceased at 1am, I lay in bed. The last time before retiring to bed, I checked WhatsApp. Surprisingly, at precisely 12am, Vikrant also wished me. I'm still conscious of that statement.

He stated: "Many many happy returns of the day PRANALI. May this year be your most marvellous year. All your dreams, all wishes will come true. Live life, queen size. My best wishes are always with you." How beautiful, isn't it?

A huge surprise awaited me in the morning. Finally, I was ready to leave for the workplace. Nimrit wasn't prepared yet. I was using the remaining time to just browse through Instagram. Our doorbell was sounded by somebody. I had to unlock the door because Nimrit was in the bedroom. Outside, a towering man was standing. I was unable to identify him. He wore a 'MARUTI SUZUKI' blouse. I assumed he was an employee of Maruti Suzuki. But why did he come here?

'Yes?' I questioned.

He questioned me back, 'Are you Pranali Sharma?'

'How in the world does this man know my name?'

'Yes, who are you?' I enquired.

'Madam, happy birthday. I'm Kabir, and I came from the Maruti Suzuki dealership to bring your property,' he introduced himself.

'My property?' I was confused.

He motioned towards the entrance and said, 'Look there.' There was a "SUZUKI ACCESS 125" sign in naval blue.

'Who's scooter is it?' I excitedly questioned.

'Yours, ma'am,' he retorted.

'Mine?' I questioned. I didn't understand his words.

'Let me be explicit, Ma'am.' He said, 'This is a gift from your parents for your birthday.'

'Really?' I questioned.

'Yes,' he answered. I phoned my father to find out what was going on. He assured me that he was cognizant of my transportation issue. So he chose to give me a scooter as a present. How thoughtful he is, I thought.

Nimrit was ecstatic when she saw my present. Once I had finished the necessary paperwork, the brand-new "SUZUKI ACCESS 125" was ultimately mine. We rode my scooter to the workplace. Sorry, mine and Nimrit's scooter. Since what belonged to me was hers and what belonged to her was also hers. Despite the fact that the workplace was our destination, the trip was fantastic. No stress over a lost transport. No sense of pressure at all. only contentment. We got to the workplace. All of the staff members stood in front of us when I opened the door. They began singing the usual dull birthday tune.

My astonishment at this revelation was complete. My first birthday since gaining my independence was that day. And everyone truly remembered my birthday. I divided up the cake among everyone. Mr. Khanna came along with us. Pratik informed me after the brief programme that the entire workplace celebrates birthdays in the same manner as they do mine. He also informed me that I wasn't a unique case. Was Pratik under any obligation to inform me about this?

When I was working, my phone called. Vikrant had called to say 'hello.' I took up a call and moved towards the balcony area.

He wished, 'Prana a happy birthday.'

'Thank you so much,' I said in return.

'Actually, I had planned to contact you at midnight, but I believed your parents might have called you.' He added, 'So I just texted you.'

'No issue. But after reading your message, I was truly amazed.'

'Wow, really?'

'Yes,' I answered.

He replied, 'Prana, I'm slightly busy right now, but I'll call you at night.'

'Okay,' I replied.

'Bye, dear,'

'Bye'. O my goodness, he called me dear, I thought, blushing. I came back to my workstation. Nimrit left Mr. Khanna's workplace and came back. For some crucial task, Mr. Khanna called her. When she turned around, she exclaimed joyfully, 'Guys, I have two pieces of news for you.'

'What?'

She smiled broadly and said, 'The first is that I got promoted.'

'Really?' Shivam exclaimed with excitement. Actually, Shivam appeared to be happier than Nimrit. And you understand the reason. Telling that is unnecessary. We all congratulated her, saying, 'That's really great news. Congratulations.' You know what, it was Shivam's first time hugging Nimrit.

'The birthday is Pranali's, but you get the present,' Pratik said in jest.

'What is the second piece of news, Nimrit?' Sonal questioned.

'The second news is that I'll be moved to our company's Bengaluru branch,' she said.

'What?' we all exclaimed in disbelief. Shivam offered more. Shivam started to utter something but stopped in the middle, 'But how can...?' The second piece of news made everyone upset. All of our joy vanished in an instant. We shared a lot of good times together. We spent a great deal of time together. But now she needed to leave. Team 7's entire roster was departing from a location far from their families. We constantly missed our relatives. We supported one another because of this.

We weren't just friends; we were more like family. As I previously mentioned, our family consisted of mother Nimrit, father Shivam, younger son Pratik, his girlfriend Sonal, and older daughter Pranali. However, our family's mother was about to leave us. Everyone remained quiet. So it was my responsibility to reignite their passion.

'Come to the hotel "sunrise" at 7 o'clock, guys. Tonight, we're throwing a celebration,' I said. Each person agreed.

My inner voice said, 'Let's also call Vikrant at the party tonight.'

'That's a really smart thought. But will he arrive?' I questioned myself.

'Do at least consult him first. Then we'll see,' my inner voice suggested me.

I wrote him, 'Are you free tonight?' I didn't want to phone him and bother him. After twenty minutes, he answered. 'Yes, but why?' he questioned.

'Actually, tonight is my birthday celebration.' I wrote, 'So, would you like to join us?'

'But will that be acceptable?'

'Of course,' I affirmed.

'Okay, I'll certainly come along with you.' He replied with a smile emoticon, 'Just send me the location and I will be there.'

After work, we went back to the apartment.

I finished my work tasks at the office, and by 6pm, I decided it was time to start getting ready for the celebration. I chose to wear a long-sleeved, formal blue dress that had been a gift from Nimrit. Nimrit herself was dressed in a stunning black gown.

One thing that put my mind at ease was that I didn't have to worry about finding a cab or facing any driver issues because I now had my own scooty. I received a text from Shivam, letting me know he was on his way. Pratik and Sonal were also making their way to our meeting spot.

With that, we all got up and left. The evening was accompanied by a gentle breeze, and the stars in the sky shone brilliantly. It was a full moon night, so the moon itself was beaming down on us. I was having a wonderful time riding my scooter, feeling the wind in my hair.

When we finally reached the Sunrise Hotel, I saw that Sonal, Pratik, and Shivam had already arrived. Surprisingly, they had got there before we did, and the celebration was off to an early start, thanks to them.

Pratik commanded, 'Let's go inside.'

I said, 'Wait, there's one more member coming.'

'Who?' Shivam enquired.

Nimrit answered, 'My brother.'

'Ohh, okay,' Pratik said.

The hero stepped out of a well-known vehicle that had just pulled into the parking lot. When I saw him, I was really surprised. I'd only seen him dressed up before, but this time, he had on a white t-shirt under his black trousers. He topped it off with a cool black leather jacket, and he looked incredibly stylish, like a Hollywood star. I couldn't help but think of Chris Hemsworth, one of my favourite Hollywood actors.

He even had on dark sunglasses, even though it was night-time. Who wears sunglasses at night? But he still looked great with his clean-shaven face, strong muscles, and broad shoulders. And the same superb figure.

He said, 'Happy birthday, Prana.'

I responded, 'Thank you so much.'

'Meet him, guys. Vikrant is my older sibling,' as Nimrit said when she introduced him to everyone.

Pratik extended his right hand and greeted Vikrant, saying, 'Nice to meet you.' Vikrant took off his glasses. Vikrant extended his palm and said, 'Me too.'

Nimrit remarked, 'And you know something, he is in "Para Special Forces".'

Pratik responded startlingly and unexpectedly, 'What?' His hands began to tremble.

Vikrant questioned him, 'What happened?'.

With a frightening grin on his face, Pratik exclaimed in relief, 'Aa.. no.. nothing.. nothing at all.'

'Good to meet you, sir. My name is Shivam.'

'Oh, so Shivam you are.' Vikrant remarked, 'I've heard a lot about you.' Shivam was quite frightened.

'Aa.. what, sir?' questioned Shivam.

'I've only heard positive things about you, so don't worry. Not like Pratik,' said Vikrant. Pratik appeared to be crying.

Nimrit introduced Sonal to Vikrant by saying, 'She is Sonal.'

'Hello, Sonal,' said Vikrant.

Sonal responded, 'Pleasure to meet you, sir.'

'Let's enter now,' I said.

We walked into the hotel's lobby, and it felt as it we had stepped into a time when fancy furniture decorated with valuable metals was seen as a sign of elegance and luxury. The hotel's inside looked modern yet simple. They used furniture in a way that felt natural, and the lighting made the place feel warm and inviting. Their idea of simplicity was evident, and I really liked it. The staff working there seemed fashionable and attractive. There was even a guitar placed on a chair in the middle of the lobby, adding a touch of charm to the whole setting.

'Why is that guitar there?' I questioned Vikrant.

'You know, I'm not this hotel's manager. So you should track him down and ask him this query,' he said. I squeezed his elbow. He mutely shrieked, 'Ouch.'

We settled in.

Sonal gave me a gift and said, 'This is for you, Prana.' Inside the gift were beautiful jhumkaas, and they sparkled in the light. Shivam then handed me a bottle of lovely perfume. Pratik, being his usual thoughtful self, gifted me a pendant that gleamed with elegance.

As I unwrapped the jewellery, I couldn't help but notice a hint of envy in Sonal's eyes. Still, I thanked them all with a grateful heart. We decided to order some paneer tikka and mushrooms to enjoy together.

While we savoured our meal, Pratik started talking in a playful and light-hearted manner, sharing jokes and stories. We all laughed and enjoyed the moment. Amidst the joy and camaraderie, I couldn't help but feel fortunate to have such wonderful friends.

To my surprise, our Para Commando, presented me with a beautiful Golden Titan Watch. I was deeply touched by his thoughtful gesture, and I knew that this watch would always remind me of him and our special bond.

As we continued to chat and share stories, I realized that these moments with my friends were priceless. Their gifts and their presence made this gathering truly memorable, and I felt a deep sense of gratitude for the love and friendship that surrounded me.

Vikrant said to me, 'Hold on a second.'

'Okay,' I retorted. We eventually heard some acoustic music. But we didn't pay it any mind. We assumed that a music system was playing it.

I recognised the voice immediately. I spun around to see who it was. Surprise! He was Vikrant. I was once again surprised by that. I was aware of how excellent his voice is. But I never imagined that he knew about sur and taal music. He used it to play the instrument as well. What a man of many talents. He pointed towards me as he was saying, 'This song is for you.'

The song was finished. Everybody applauded for him. He came and sat besides me.

I murmured to Vikrant, 'I won't forget this moment. Thank you.' He nodded.

A tremendous meal awaited us, and the food was absolutely delicious. After settling the bill, I expressed my gratitude to everyone for making my birthday so memorable. With heartfelt goodbyes, we headed back to our house.

As soon as we arrived home, I was so exhausted that I practically collapsed into bed. It had been an incredibly special day filled with joy and celebration. However, there was a cloud of unease hanging over me because I had received some troubling news.

Nimrit, my dearest friend and housemate, had been transferred. It hit me hard that I would have to spend the next 30 days without her by my side. Nimrit was not just a friend; she was like family to me. We shared a unique bond and a deep attachment. The thought of facing my days without her was almost unbearable.

Lost in my thoughts and worries, I drifted into unconsciousness, unaware of the world around me. I couldn't help but wonder how I would cope with her absence and what my days would be like without my closest confidante and companion.

...

Finally, the time had come for Nimrit to leave from our workplace and join the Bengaluru branch of our business. A month had flown by in no time. We tried to have fun together during those 30 days without getting into any pointless arguments. But the truth is, we are female. And these pointless fights are an integral component of our daily lives.

Nimrit's modest send-off celebration was organised by Mr. Khanna. merely to enhance the significance and memory of her final day of employment. I handed her the keys and reclined in the backseat as I waited to enter the office. Everyone was already there when we arrived.

When word spread that it was her last day at that workplace, everyone became upset. Everyone in our workplace loved her, including me. Everyone found it extremely difficult to embrace the reality that 'she will not work with us anymore.'

That day, she was incredibly sensitive. You know what, though, we have to make some compromises in order to move closer to our goal. Since joy following the realisation of our goal is greater than sorrow as a result of these sacrifices. She was promoted. Both her status and her pay had grown. Her entire existence would soon change. In Bengaluru, she had to finish the next stage of her existence. Everything was novel to her—the location, the people, everything. But I was confident that she would quickly become accustomed to it.

Although Vikrant was very upset, he was pleased that her sister was promoted to a higher position in her business. The fact that Nimrit was hired in the same city as her brother's posting was actually a huge accident. because troops aren't always stationed close to their loved ones. Living in the same metropolis was truly a stroke of luck and coincidence for them both.

Shivam was the person in the workplace who was most upset. I questioned him about his wellbeing. He told me he was all right while lying. He wasn't, though. His one and only love was leaving him and travelling far away. He still hadn't declared his affection for Nimrit. However, he was still very protective of her.

It was time for the farewell function following our business hours. However, one individual was absent their. Shivam had vanished. The first person to note his absence was Nimrit. She muttered 'Where is Shiv?' in my ear.

I said, 'I don't know. Wait I will find out.'

I pondered his possible location. So I gave him a call. On the balcony, he claimed to be. I then stood in line to enter the balcony. He was standing on the terrace's apex and gazing up. Sky was overcast. I could feel how he was. I understood his emotions. I moved slowly in his direction. He appeared to be truly disoriented.

'Why are you in this place? The programme has already started,' I declared.

'Yes... I know,' he retorted.

I questioned, 'So why are you here?'

He paused before finally responding, 'Because... I don't know.'

I asked, my eyes fixed on the clouds, 'Listen Shivam, why don't you confess to her?'

'Because I'm not sure of how she'll respond.' Looking down, he asked, 'What if she refuses me and excludes me from her life forever?'

'I'm not sure how she'll respond, Shivam, but I think you should confess your love for her. She won't do anything you are thinking on her doing. That is my promise. If something goes awry, I'll take care of it. So stop being a baby and start behaving like a man. Let's leave now; Nimrit is waiting.'

'What?'

'Yes,' I responded, 'She is the one who noticed your absence and she only sent me here.' He grinned. 'Come with me now,' I said.

Nimrit was overjoyed when Shivam arrived. The programme went on. Shivam declined to comment on Nimrit, considering that he was aware of his inability to control his feelings.

Nimrit finally stood up to talk. 'Good Afternoon, everybody. I'm stunned, to be perfectly honest. First of all, I want to appreciate you for organising this lovely event. I started working here two years ago. I recently received a raise, so I must travel to Bengaluru.

'I'm taking a lot of information with me when I leave today. Working here has been a wonderful educational opportunity, and I am appreciative of the abilities I have gained. I believe that spending each day here with you all has improved my overall well-being. I've improved my ability to accept criticism, praise, and guidance. I used to struggle with these three things, but now I feel like I can use them in a variety of circumstances. In order to produce a fantastic outcome, I've also learned to be open-minded, respect other people's views, and take into account other ideas in addition to mine.

'I want to appreciate Mr. Khanna once more. He gave me a lot of advice and support. My roommate and best friend Pranali. Shivam, Pratik, and Sonal make up my squad of seven. I appreciate your assistance and support, everyone. I'm grateful for this farewell celebration and eager to learn about your future successes. Thank you thanks a lot.'

She was praised by everyone. She gave everyone a smile and wished them farewell.

...

Shivam requested a coffee meeting with Nimrit after the programme was over. Nimrit agreed. I went back to my room by myself after Shivam assured me that he would leave Nimrit. I was curious to hear Shivam's response. I was hoping everything goes well.

After a while, Nimrit came back. She gave a cheerful vibe. I assumed everything was fine and was very curious to find out.

I eagerly questioned, 'What happened, what did he say?'

She responded, 'I'm so exhausted right now that I'm going to take a bath first, then I'll inform you.' My desire was growing as she spoke. She washed too slowly. Finally, she came back. 'Ok, now inform me. What just happened?'

'All right, I'll tell you.' She said, 'Let me have a cup of water first.'

Angrily, I uttered, 'Nimrit.'

She exclaimed, 'Ha.. ha.. ha..' with a Dayan laugh. 'Okay, now please be patient.'

'Please tell me,' I pleaded naively.

'Listen, now. He drove me to Mongivilla Café. You know, it's really a great café,' she said.

'I have no desire to hear how excellent café Mongivilla is. Tell me now precisely what transpired between you two.'

'We first grabbed a seat.' I was asked, "What will you have?" by him. I retorted, 'Umm.. just hot coffee." "Please, two hot coffees," he commanded. There was a lengthy pause following that. Although he seemed very anxious, I knew he had to tell me something.

"Shivam," I uttered. "Would you mind telling me something?"

"Yes"

"Then tell me, please."

"Nimrit, the thing is....."

He was cut off by the waiter, "Your coffee, sir."

He said to the server, "Thank you."

I pleaded to him to go on.

"Nimrit, the thing is..."

"What is that?"

He said, "Nimrit, I love you." I was taken aback. My pupils bulged wide. "Yes, Nimrit, I adore you so," he continued. Once more, there was a lengthy pause.

"Why didn't you tell me earlier," I naively questioned.

"I was terrified"

"Who or what?"

"I truly love you, Nimrit. I was therefore afraid that you would dismiss me. What if I'm blocked by you? Many more queries came to mind. I never told you that I loved you," he said.

"How can you conceive of everything on your own, idiot? Who informed you that I would act in such a way? Who informed you I would block you, exactly?" I asked, "Who informed you that I don't like you?"

Surprised, he inquired, "What?"

His palm in mine, I said, "I also adore you, Shiv. But you waited too long to admit it. I don't know when we'll meet again because I'm going tomorrow." His eyes started to tear up. I continued, "But I promise you one thing: I am only yours, and very shortly we will get married."'

'What do you mean by that, Nimrit?' I questioned.

'Yes,' Nimrit affirmed.

I teased, 'Means you also loved him, right?'

'Aa…' she cried out, 'I have to pack my bags,' and walked out.

...

We received a major surprise at night. The length of our doorbell. Guess what, Pratik, Shivam, and Sonal stood there when I opened the door.

I questioned, 'What are you doing here at this time?'

'You step aside.' Pratik responded, 'We are here for Nimrit,' and pushed me. Nimrit entered the foyer. Nimrit questioned, 'What happened guys, why are you here?'

'You know, Nimrit, this is our final night as Team 7 together,' Pratik said.

'So,' Shivam added, 'We are here to make it more memorable.'

Sonal added, 'And we are staying here tonight.'

Pratik yelled, 'Aaj raat sona mana hai (sleeping tonight is not allowed)!'

Sonal said, 'We will sing, dance, eat, drink, and enjoy the entire night.' Nimrit and I were both in awe. But they had a point. Since it was Team 7's final night together, it had to be special. So the celebration started.

We started with a DJ night. After we collapsed from exhaustion, Pratik brought us pizza and beer. We then began playing Antaxari. I have no idea when we went to sleep.

I opened my eyes to find Nimrit standing by a window. Shivam eventually approached her. I pretended to be asleep because I wanted to see what would happen next. They gave each other an embrace. For me, it came as quite a surprise. I kept playing because I didn't wanted to ruin their ecstatic moment. They amazed me more when they kissed each other, when idiot Pratik ruined the occasion with his remark, 'Wah.. kya scene hai (Ohh.. what a scene)'. Nimrit and Shivam felt ashamed. I began to beat Pratik along with Sonal.

...

At 1pm, Nimrit had reporting. After waking up, we had brunch as a group. I phoned Vikrant to check on whether or not he would be sending Nimrit. However, he claimed that he was unable to attend because he had a crucial meeting. Nimrit made the decision to first travel to her house, remain there for a few days, and then join her new job in Bengaluru.

We got to the airport. On Shivam's motorcycle, Nimrit arrived. It was time to say our last goodbyes. So we gave each other hugs, said farewell in a friendly manner, and wished her a long and healthy life. But just as I was about to enter the terminal, she walked up to me and said, 'You know something? I think Vikkie bhaiyya loves you back,'

'Back? What does she mean when she said "back"?,' asked myself.

We remained there for a while before going back to our separate rooms.

The space felt bare. For the previous five months, Nimrit was with me. She and I slept in the same bed. She has since vanished. Vikrant was the one who could comprehend my feelings, so I called him at night. In reality, every girl requires a male friend with whom she feels comfortable sharing anything. It's not essential to be in a relationship. Her closest friends could be him. He must be trustworthy, which is ultimately what matters most.

Girls do not readily or easily express their emotions to any guy, and if they do, it means that person is very special to them. You guys must therefore uphold their confidence. Anyhow, let's get to the tale. I felt fantastic after talking to Vikrant. We were getting closer to one another every day.

I could no longer tolerate the loneliness. I then asked my mother to come remain with me. Mother, who adores her children dearly, is the only person who is aware of the mood swings of her children. It is clear that she was overjoyed to see me again. She had many sweets and other food products with her when she arrived here. One thing I forgot to tell you. My mother's name is Anjali Sharma.

'Prano, I will make your favourite biryani for you.' she always knew what I wanted.

'Why don't we welcome your friend Vikrant to dinner tonight, Prano?' she enquired. I told her everything I knew about Vikrant. She didn't mind that I was so close to him, unlike other mothers. She actually has a very modern mind-set. She encouraged me in every choice I made. I am extremely fortunate to have her.

Vikrant accompanied us since he was free that evening. Mother was overjoyed to see him. She was extremely happy that I had made a companion who supports our country. Vikrant loved the way she treated him like her own child. Mom was avidly enquiring about his military experiences. She appeared to be attending his interview, though, mothers are mothers, whatever.

The biryani had been made. Mom gave it to us both. Its fragrance permeated the entire apartment. Without a question, it was improved. First mouthful was taken by Vikrant. He must have received a prize for his excessive acting at the time, in my opinion.

He said, 'Aunty, you make biryani that is far more delectable than you daughter.' Mom ascended Mount Everest right away.

Mom stood by my side for a week. She frequently asked Vikrant over for dinner. Additionally, this active fighter always found time for it. I had no issues with it. They became the best of pals in just a week. Now, I was having a lot of trouble with this. They began treating me like I was a statue of a girl kept on a couch that was lifeless. They gave me the cold shoulder. Vikrant was making my own mother ignore me. And I'm not going to ever forget what he did. And my mother was attempting to separate me from my best friend. I will never be able to pardon her for that.

'Mom, you must now return to Mumbai,' I informed her. Dad was there alone, and it was clear that he missed his one and only wife. I felt sorry for him. Nobody who could take care of him was present. Now don't call me "Papa ki pari (angel of dad)" I too developed emotional stability. And so she went. Vikrant, however, clearly missed her more than I did.

I still recall how irresponsible I was when my mother was around. I used to get up an hour or so before work. My mother used to make breakfast and pack my lunch. She waited for me when I got back. She washed all my garments, kept my apartment tidy, and did a lot more for me. But after she left, I really missed her.

❑

CHAPTER 5

Siddharth Khanna

SEPTEMBER 2015, NEWTOWN, KOLKATA

I was working in the office when Mr. Khanna summoned me, Pratik, Shivam and Sonal to his cabin. When we arrived, we noticed a tall, dashing man standing close to Mr. Khanna. He had silky shining hair and well-trimmed beards, and he was clothed in a full-sleeved baby pink shirt and grey trousers. His appearance was enhanced by his thick eyebrows.

'Sonal, who is he?' I inquired.

'I didn't know,' she said in response.

'Meet him, guys. Siddharth Khanna is my son,' Mr. Khanna declared. 'He will also be a new member of team 7 and its leader,' he continued. Since he was smart and Mr. Khanna informed us that he had his own startup in Australia, I was actually very excited to work for him. He greeted us and we returned to our task after that. Siddharth sat down next to me.

He said, 'Hello friends, can we get together for coffee after work?'

'Why not?' we all asked.

We finished our task and then met in the cafe. For us, Siddharth requested five coffees.

'So let me first give a brief introduction of myself. Siddharth Khanna here. You can call me Sid. I completed my secondary education in Pune before moving to the United States to conclude my undergraduate studies. After that, I went to Australia to start my own company. But my father told me that he requires me to be here. I'm here, then.' He appeared to have a magnanimous heart. He lacked all forms of attitude. This trait appeals to me. We exchanged phone numbers, and I then go back to my apartment.

After finishing my work, I had dinner, went to bed, and scrolled through Instagram. 'Hey, it's Sid,' said the WhatsApp message that appeared on my phone.

'Hi,' I replied.

'Dinner?'

'Just. You?'

'Just,' he answered.

On that night, we talked a lot. I won't go into the remainder of it, though. I learned during our conversation that there were many things that were alike between us. We share the same birthday. Numerous things about our tastes are comparable. But he did say that we could become excellent friends. Yes, I agree it.

The following day, while Sid had not arrived yet, I was the Café. In fact, he invited me to join him for coffee yesterday. I believed it to be a brilliant idea. We'll get to know each other better. He seated down in front of me after entering the cafe.

He said, 'I'm sorry for arriving late.'

I retorted, 'No no, it's all right.'

He enquired, 'What would you like to order?'

I simply said, 'I'll take vanilla ice cream.'

'All right, I'll take the same. Two vanilla ice creams,' he ordered.

'Inform me a little about yourself.' He inquired, 'What are your hobbies?'

'Singing, dancing, book perusing, etc. Yours?' I enquired.

'Well, I enjoy writing poetry.'

'Really?' I pressed.

'Yes, I write novels as well.' He questioned, 'Would you like to read it?'

'Off course,' I answered.

'Okay, I'll give it to you tomorrow.'

'Thanks,' I said.

'You're welcome,' he retorted with a grin. We got our order.

'I believe we were meant to meet,' he said with a gentle grin.

'How,' I questioned.

'See, our work is the same, and our interests and preferences are the same'

'Yes, that's true. We were meant to meet,' I concluded with a smile.

He heard about my relatives from me. He shared some of his encounters with me. But I refrained from telling him about Vikrant, and he skipped the question. I went back home.

The following day, Sid gave me a copy of his book 'Can we meet for one last time?' After perusing the title, I was incredibly eager and impatient to start reading. But why the last time, I questioned.

'After finishing this novel, you'll know the answer,' he said.

...

I was reading the book, Sid had gifted me which entitled, 'Can we meet for one last time?' There were only going to be 10 papers left. I began reading because I was eager to see how it ended.

Finally finished. It took me just 6 days. I phoned Sid to let him know I had finished the book and had enjoyed it a lot.

'Can we get coffee tomorrow?' Just the two of us?' he questioned.

'Sure.'

I was waiting for Sid at the Hard Rock Café, the following day. It is a well-known waterfront restaurant that offers delectable fare and beverages in addition to renowned music memorabilia. It was when I heard the shocking report on the television in the restaurant.

"In a shocking turn of events, a well-known businessman in Delhi was found dead in his residence yesterday, sending shockwaves throughout the city. The incident has left the public in a state of distress, and the authorities are now investigating a potentially significant lead – the presence of a rogue soldier, Captain Prithvi, near the crime scene.

The victim, identified as Mr. Ramesh Kapoor, a renowned figure in the Delhi business community, was discovered lifeless in his upscale residence in the heart of the city. According to initial reports, Mr. Kapoor's body bore signs of violence, and the cause of death is being treated as a homicide. This gruesome discovery has sparked an immediate police response, and a murder investigation is underway.

Crucially, nearby security cameras captured a figure believed to be Captain Prithvi, a former soldier who has recently been linked to several unlawful activities. In the surveillance footage, Captain Prithvi can be seen near the vicinity of Mr. Kapoor's residence around the time of the murder.

Law enforcement agencies have not ruled out the possibility of Captain Prithvi's involvement in the businessman's murder.

Although the exact nature of the connection between Mr. Kapoor and Captain Prithvi remains unclear, the circumstantial evidence is cause for concern.

Assistant Police Commissioner, Aparna Sharma, commented on the situation, stating, "We are treating this case with the utmost seriousness. Captain Prithvi is a person of interest in this investigation, given the evidence we have at this stage. However, we are exploring all possible leads and conducting a thorough inquiry."

The Delhi Police have issued an appeal to the public for any information related to the murder or the whereabouts of Captain Prithvi. Anyone with knowledge of the incident or Captain Prithvi's current location is urged to come forward and assist with the ongoing investigation.

The investigation into the murder of Mr. Ramesh Kapoor is still in its early stages, and the presence of Captain Prithvi near the crime scene has raised significant questions. As the authorities work diligently to unravel the circumstances surrounding this tragic event, the city remains on edge, hoping for justice and closure in this high-profile case."

Captain Prithvi?

Who the hell is this guy?

As I listened to the news report about the gruesome murder of a prominent businessman in Delhi and the possible involvement of a rogue soldier, Captain Prithvi, a shiver of unease ran down my spine. Being an outsider to the city, I had no prior knowledge of Captain Prithvi or the victim, but the shocking revelation still left me with a sense of dread.

I was thinking about all this when I saw Sid approaching me. He sat down and we placed a two-coffee order.

'The novel is fantastic,' I said, 'Every scene moved my heart.' I added.

'Thank you.' He inquired, 'Can I tell you something?'

'Of course'.

'Actually, this is my tale,' he said, shocking me. 'When I was 18, I had a crush on a woman called Priya. She was a lovely but reserved young lady. Her innocence appealed to me. We became friends. We gradually grown close to one another. But after that, we began to love one another.

'As I began to know her, I discovered that there were many things concealed behind her cheerful countenance. I told her that I would stand by her side no matter what and that I would always make her happy. She believed me.

'Everything was proceeded well until my dad was informed about Priya. She was a destitute, lower-caste girl, and as you are aware, I come from a wealthy household. Her mother had her own finest parlour, and her father worked as a watchman. Dad warned me not to approach her. How then could I? I've always loved her. However, one day he discovered us in a field. My father struck me for the first time. He threatened to murder Priya if I ever tried to speak with her again. And I was absolutely certain that he could. How could I allow this to happen? So I instructed Priya to disregard me.

'My promises and all her hopes were broken. I'll never be able to forget that. She made a valiant effort to persuade me. "Please don't leave me, I can't live without you," she pleaded. "We've had dreams about having children. Right, we've always wanted to be together. Why then do you leave me now? Sid, don't give up." I can still hear them in my ears: "I can't live without you."

"My father wishes me to pursue my education in America," I told her. She wished to see me one final time. A final occasion. So, "Can we meet for one last time?" is the title of the novel.'

I made a concerted to forget about her, but I couldn't. I once received a call from Priya asking, "How are you Sid?"

"Fine. You?"

"I'm getting married to Vikas next month," she said, shattering my heart into countless fragments. "Sid, please take action. I have no desire to wed him. But I'm being forced to do it by my family.

Sid, I adore you. If you don't take action, I'll have to wed Vikas." Before me, the wrong thing was occurring. Nothing could be done by me.' Sid was motionless.

'What happened next?' I questioned.

'That's it, she got married to Vikas,' he said after pausing briefly.

'And you done nothing?' I asked, he casted a low glance that indicated "no."

'Sid, I've read this book. I am aware of your struggles. This is not someone's fault, in my opinion. I believe you two weren't meant to be together. She is now joyful. Therefore, the time has come for you to move on with your existence. You are a charming, astute, and wise man. I think that you will find someone unique waiting for you.'

However, one thing that continued to puzzle me was why he had chosen to confess his past relationship with me. We weren't particularly close, not the kind of friends who typically share their deepest secrets. So, I couldn't help but wonder why he had decided to do so.

...

The night was wrapped in a blanket of darkness, and I decided to reach out to Vikrant, eager to connect with him after a day filled with unsettling news. I dialled his number, and when he answered, I couldn't help but inquire about his day.

'Hey, Vikrant, how was your day?' I asked, my voice tinged with concern.

His response was measured, 'Good, I guess.'

His choice of words didn't go unnoticed, and I probed further, seeking to understand. 'I guess?' I inquired, hoping for more insight into his day.

Vikrant's voice carried a weight of responsibility as he explained, 'Yes, I had many meetings today regarding the security of the city.'

I acknowledged his demanding schedule with a simple ‘Okay,’ recognizing the crucial role he played in safeguarding the city.

Curiosity then led me to bring up the news report I had heard earlier in the day. ‘Do you know about that rogue soldier, what is his name, Captain Prithvi?’ I questioned, wondering if Vikrant had insights into the matter.

Vikrant’s response carried a tone of familiarity and a hint of history. ‘Yeah, no one knows him better than me,’ he admitted.

Surprised by his assertion, I asked, ‘How?’ My curiosity was aroused, and I leaned in to listen.

Vikrant began to reveal the enigmatic past he shared with Captain Prithvi, describing him as a young, dashing, intelligent, and sharp soldier. They had been comrades, and Vikrant had thought of him as a kindred spirit. ‘It was always amazing to spend time with him,’ Vikrant reminisced, a hint of nostalgia in his voice. ‘We were friends, so I taught him everything I had learned. I thought he would be one who would come between nation’s peace, and the terrorists of the nation.’

I listened intently, absorbing this glimpse into a shadowy past, but the narrative took a chilling turn as Vikrant revealed the shocking truth. ‘He killed 6 innocent Kashmiri civilians and betrayed us,’ he disclosed, leaving me utterly astounded.

My voice trembled as I asked, ‘What? What was the reason?’

Vikrant’s response was laden with the weight of the past. ‘No one knows. I tried to stop him, but I failed,’ he admitted. The memory of their confrontation seemed to haunt him. ‘I still remember his cold eyes when we faced each other.’

My mind raced with questions, and I couldn’t help but wonder about the capabilities of this rogue soldier. ‘Is he more formidable than Vikrant?’ I pondered to myself.

Vikrant continued, offering insight into the ongoing manhunt for Captain Prithvi. ‘From that day, he began to be considered a rogue soldier. He was seen in different places in India, but we are yet unable to capture him.’

He paused for a moment, his voice resolute. 'And you know something, only I know how he thinks. That's why the one who will capture and kill him is me,' he asserted with conviction.

A moment of silence lingered between us, and I understood that the weight of his past experiences and the mission to bring this rogue soldier to justice weighed heavily on Vikrant's shoulders.

As the call ended, I was left with a profound understanding of the complexities and challenges that Vikrant faced, a world shrouded in shadows and secrets, and the unwavering determination to confront his past.

❑

CHAPTER 6

The Heart's Enchantment

OCTOBER 2015, NEWTOWN, KOLKATA,

The worst day of my existence. It was a Saturday, and as usual, Mr. Khanna gave me a tonne of paperwork to complete. I had to work on it over time in order to finish it, which caused severe fatigue. I finished my job at 8 o'clock. I was lucky to have my own scooter.

I had finished my office duties and was going home. My scooty broke down as I was travelling. I attempted to figure out why, and when I did, I discovered that the gas tank was completely empty.

'Nooooo……', I screamed loudly.

Hopefully no one could hear it.

I don't know why, but that night the motorway seemed incredibly unsettling. There weren't any more cars passing. I was still 2kilometers away from my apartment. I parked my scooter at a nearby parking area because I didn't think it was safe to ask for a lift, then I began to walk to my room.

I was frightened by the blackness and silence. So I made the decision to contact Vikrant. If he is open, he will provide me with company.

After 7 or 8 rings, he answered the phone.

When he picked up the phone, he immediately inquired, 'Hey Prano, how are you?'

I tiredly retorted, 'Not well.'

'What happened?' I told him the whole tale, concluding, 'Today is really worse.'

'What? So, where are you now?' he questioned.

'Still 2 kilometers away from my apartment.'

He replied, 'Wait there, I'll send someone to get you,'

'No no, there is no need,' I declared.

'Are you sure?'

'Yes'

'Okay then'.

I was being wounded by the piercing air. Unfortunately, I chose to wear my best black sleeveless skirt, which turned out to be the worst outfit choice of the day. However, the sky was as gorgeous as it always is. The stars were brilliant. The moon had a distinctive glamour shine.

I questioned Vikrant, 'Hey, where are you right now?'

'Room. Then why?'

'Will you kindly join me on the terrace?' I requested.

'Okay, but why? '

'Come no', I said innocently.

'Okay. Just a moment,' he urged.

After a short while, he said, 'Ok, now tell me.'

I enquired, 'Can you see the stars?'

'Yes, they are beautiful, but not more so than you.'

I laughed and said, 'Ha.. ha., joke of the day.'

'No, I'm not joking.'

'Oh, okay. Thank you,' I said.

'You know what,' he said, 'I prefer this darkness to light.'

'Oh, and why is that?' I excitedly enquired.

'You know, there is calmness and peace in it,'

'Ya'

'And in the dark, no one is different; everyone is the same.'

'Correct,' I replied.

'You know what I do when I'm upset?'

'What?'

'I go to the terrace, put earbuds in my ears, play old love tunes, and look up at the stars,' he said.

'How lovely!'

'Yes,' he answered.

'When I look at the sky, I think of my childhood,' I said. 'You know something, when I was a child, in our colony, we all used to play hide and seek at first,' she said. 'Then we used to play Antaxari after supper. After that, my grandmother would tell us scary tales that she claimed were true' I continued with a grin.

'What? True scary tales?'

'Those were some really lovely days,' I said.

From behind me, I could hear one motorbike. It became clear that it was KTM when I turned. After approaching me, it abruptly halted. This KTM guy inquired, 'May I drop you?' I couldn't tell who he was because his helmet obscured his visage.

I answered him, 'No thanks.'

He urged Pranali, 'Come on, I'll drop you.' I don't know how he knows my name.

I enquired, 'How do you know me?'

I overheard Vikrant on my cell phone asking, 'What is going on, Prano?'

I told him, 'Hold on a second.' The KTM man took off his headgear. And he was, in fact, AKASH. Akash who? Already forgotten? He is the one who asked me out at the bus stop. He is the only individual I truly despise.

'You recognised me?' he enquired.

'You?' I snapped, 'What are you doing here?'

'I was simply driving by when I realised that my future bride needed my assistance. I therefore came here to assist you,' and upon hearing that, my thoughts completely lost control. My outrage grew.

'What the hell?' I asked furiously, 'Who knows what you are talking about.'

'Wait, wait, wait.' He said shamelessly, 'First we will go to your room, then we will talk.'

I said, 'No way.' Call was still ringing.

He yelled, 'Come on, Pranali,' and seized my right palm. That was adequate. I gave him a firm smack in the face.

I yelled, 'Go to hell,' and then I began to move. I hung up the phone and put my phone in my purse. He may leave now, but I was mistaken.

He put his bike aside and approached me. He gave me a backhanded smack and said, 'How dare you.' My head struck the ground after I fell on the sidewalk. I lost consciousness.

I don't know what happened, but when I woke up, I was in a dark room. It was so black that I couldn't see anything around me. My wrists and legs were tied down, and there was a piece of cloth covering my mouth. I felt really scared, and I was sweating profusely. I couldn't understand what was happening to me or why it was happening.

'Oh God, please save me,' I cried out in prayer. My only chance there was in him. When we notice that all doorways are shut, we act in that manner. We pray that he will rescue us. I was forced to turn to God in prayer.

When I was crying about my fortune, I heard some noise. Someone walked into the space. I grew more frightened. I discover that he was Akash once more when the lights were switched on. All of this was his doing. He was grinning wickedly. He approached me and took off the piece of cloth covering my lips.

'Why are you acting in this way? I beg you. Please leave me. What do you want from me?' I said yelling.

He said, 'You, I want you.'

'Leave me alone, please.' His smile returned.

'You know what, if you had accepted my love, none of this would have occurred. However, you didn't. You were courting that soldier the entire time,' I was surprised to learn. 'I was watching every move you made. You understand how I felt, right? I love a lady who is seeing someone else. Later, I'll deal with him.' He began to approach me and said, 'First I will deal with you.' In his gaze, I could see the devil.

'Help, help, help!' I screamed as loud as I could. But, I suppose, nobody paid it any attention. He brutally seized my visage. I was attempting to break free of his hold, but it was beyond my power. Once more, I lost consciousness.

I discovered myself on the bed when I opened my eyes. I was in my room, lying on my bed. I felt stunned. Was it just a dream? I felt stunned. I was attempting to recall what had occurred. It seemed to be a hallucination. My eyes immediately began to tear up as soon as I recalled the entire situation.

I got out of bed and glanced at myself in the mirror. I had some scratches on my torso, and my dress had some tears in it. Not a nightmare, exactly. From the entryway, I could hear some noise. I arrived at the hall to find out what it was. When I saw one tall man sleeping on a sofa, I was terrified. Looking at him gave me goosebumps. He wore a cloth over his face, so I couldn't tell who he was. Is he Akash once more? He is who? A thief?

I chose a flowerpot and decided to strike his skull. I slowly began to form a line in his direction. When he took off his handkerchief and opened his eyes, I lifted a flowerpot to strike him.

He was Vikrant.

'Vikrant?' I surprised myself by asking, 'What the hell are you doing here?' I tripped over a flowerpot, breaking it into a hundred fragments.

'What exactly am I doing here? Do you not recall what transpired the previous evening?'

'No,' I answered.

'All right, I'll tell you. I'll return after first going to my house,'

'No, first tell me what happened last evening'

'Settle down; I'll be back shortly.' He declared, 'In reality, I have a fantastic plan for today.

'What plan? Please make it obvious no,' I said innocently.

'All right I will tell you. First sit here calmly'.

I said, 'All right,' and sat down on the couch. He was in front of me.

'Now inform,' I irritably said.

'So, last night while we were on a call, I heard a guy's voice, and it sounded like you were arguing with him. It got me worried because I thought something might be wrong. We ended our call after I heard you shouting, and that made me even more uneasy. So, I made a decision to come and check on you.

'But when I came here, to this place, I found that the entrance was locked from the outside. That was a clear sign that something was definitely not right.

'I contacted my group and asked them to help me trace your phone number. And guess where they traced your phone's location?

You were out in the woods, far away from the city. When I got to that location, I noticed an old house. You were inside that house, as my team had informed me.

'I tried to open the door, but it was locked from the inside. I had no other option but to break it open. Here's where it gets intense—my instincts told me that as soon as I entered that building, someone might try to attack me from behind. And you know what? My instincts were right.

'When I turned around, I saw a man pointing a stick at me. I quickly grabbed that stick and, well, let's just say he tried to fight me. But I need to tell you, I'm a Para Commando, so it was like a warm-up for me. I hit him on the forehead, and he passed out.'

'One woman was unconscious when I spun around and found her in the corner of the room. I realised she was YOU when I got near to her. You had a terrible appearance. You had rope tied around your wrists and legs. I was done then. That was enough to bring me to a full simmer. No one can harm my friend because I am Captain Vikrant Shergil of the Para Commandos.'

I responded, 'What? What happened then?'

'I made that idiot aware that the human body contains 206 bones, all of which can break at once and cause excruciating pain.'

'You did that?'

'Of course, I brought you here after that. While you were unconscious, you were saying, "Please help me; stay with me," even though I had already made the decision to leave. I therefore made the decision to remain. You're now asking me what the heck I'm doing in this place. Good, very good.'

I was stunned after listening him. My hands, knees, and feet were all shaking. My eyes began to well up with tears.

'What happened, Prano?' he naively questioned. I sobbed, blotting away my tears, 'Nothing.' He was sympathetic to what I was going through. He drew near and gently grasped my face.

'Prano, you are a brave girl. Strong girl never tears, either. So please cease crying,' he said, wiping away my tears. 'And no matter what happens, I will always be by your side,' he added. 'I'll always be there for you. I'm always here to keep you safe. I'll defend you till the very end. Leave it to my name.'

His words, 'Leave it to my name,' deeply affected me. I lost all sense of reality and gave him a tight embrace, really close. I pleaded with him to never leave me. Actually, I had no idea what I was saying or doing at the moment.

He rested his right palm on my head and said, 'I'll be there for you Pranali, I swear.'

Wow, what a time that was.

In that one hug, the anguish I had been holding in burst forth. In his arms, I felt incredibly secure, content, and pleased. I had the impression that I was looking for this. He assured me that he would be there for me no matter what happened by placing his hand on my head.

I eventually regained my wits. I recoiled and took two steps back. For a brief moment, we were quiet.

'Now, start to be fresh.' He broke the hush by saying, 'We're leaving.'

'Where?'

'Just be prepared. I will be back in 2 hours,' he advised before walking away. I was interested in our destination.

'Are we going on a date? And if it's a date, I need to make a lot more preparations,' I told myself.

...

Our first official date had me feeling a mix of emotions – excitement and nervousness all at once. I had those classic "butterflies in my stomach" because, unlike most girls, I was about to go on a date with a Para Commando, Captain Vikrant.

I freshened up as per Vikrant's orders, even though my body still ached from past wounds. But none of that mattered now because Vikrant's embrace had a magical way of healing not just my physical wounds but also my heart and mind.

The big question was, what should I wear? It was our first date, and Vikrant and I were going out alone for the very first time. I opened my closet, filled with many beautiful exquisite, but choosing the right one was a dilemma. I found myself missing Nimrit, my friend, at that moment. I remembered Vikrant once saying that I looked stunning in pink. So, after much pondering, I decided on a long, pink Anarkali dress.

Thankfully, I had a facial just two days before, so my complexion had a natural glow. Vikrant had also mentioned his love for the beauty of nature, so I kept my makeup simple – just pink lipstick on my lips and a touch of powder on my forehead. I gave myself one final look in the mirror, and felt satisfied with my choice.

My inner voice proclaimed, 'Vikrant is going to die.'

'Thank you,' I replied.

I came off as foolish. My phone began to vibrate. Vikrant made the call.

'Ready?' he questioned.

'Yes'

'Then hurry up. I'm waiting by the parking lot.'

'Just a moment,' I retorted.

Even though it was rainy season, the day was bright. The breeze was warm. I left my apartment sometime around 11am. In the parking lot, where Vikrant was waiting for me, I went. He was staring in the opposite direction as I was. His huge bums, if you'll pardon the expression, were all I could see of him. Surprisingly, he matched my frock with a pink full-sleeved shirt.

What an amazing chance, huh?

Certainly, here's a more elaborate version:

I began, drawing near to him. I gently placed my hand on his shoulders, prompting him to swivel around to face me. There was a momentary pause as he seemed taken aback.

He swivelled around. He paused before saying, 'Okay,' and then he began gazing at me with his eyes wide open. His jaw was also open.

My inner voice said, 'I told you, he's going to die.'

I said, 'Vikrant.'

'You, Aa..a.,' he stammered, his eyes widened, and his jaw hung slightly open.

Puzzled, I inquired, 'What?'

Despite his initial struggle with words, he managed to say, 'You are looking really beautiful, Prana.'

I graciously accepted the compliment, responding with a simple, 'Thank you.'

We embarked on our journey on my scooter, as per Vikrant's request. He took the driver's seat, and I settled into the back. My right palm rested on his shoulder as we made our way.

Curiosity got the better of me, and I couldn't resist asking, 'Where are we going?'

Vikrant, with a hint of excitement, replied, 'To a theatre.' The anticipation of our destination filled the air as we drove along, ready to enjoy an evening together.

"Pixels" was the movie.

After that we queued towards hotel "Royal Bengal" for lunch. We both craved spicy cuisine, so we both placed an order for "Chicken Kolhapuri". If you enjoy spicy food and are not a vegetarian, you must taste it.

As the sun slowly descended, we decided to visit the "Victoria Memorial," an impressive marble structure nestled in the heart of Kolkata, dedicated to Queen Victoria. It was a remarkable experience. The Victoria Memorial Museum housed an impressive array of 25 rooms, each with its unique treasures.

Among the highlights were the central hall, the sculpture gallery, the arms and armoury gallery, the Kolkata museum, the royal gallery, the national leader's gallery, the portrait gallery, and the gallery of portraits. Additionally, the museum boasted a collection of rare and antiquarian books, including volumes on Thumri music, illustrated writings of William Shakespeare, and tales from the Arabian Nights. We also admired various portraits of Queen Victoria and Prince Albert.

After exploring the museum, we ventured into the courtyard area. There, we discovered statues, a graceful bridge, and a majestic statue of Queen Victoria seated on her throne. We took our time to soak in the ambience before finding a comfortable spot to rest.

Our gaze turned westward, where the sun was preparing to set. The evening, often considered the most enchanting time of day, unfolded before us. As the sun dipped lower, the sky transformed into a mesmerising canvas, painted with hues ranging from vibrant orange to vivid pink. The golden disc of the sun gradually faded, leaving behind its final rays. It was a spectacle that held the power to alleviate any tension, made even more soothing by the gentle breeze that rustled through the air.

As the stars began to twinkle and the moon had already emerged, we found ourselves pondering the calming effect of twilight. It's a time that offers respite for the mind, allowing it to momentarily escape the worries of the past and the anxieties of the future.

And so, in that tranquil moment, we both sat there, peacefully immersed in the beauty of the fading sun and the soothing embrace of twilight.

Breaking the silence, Vikrant inquired, 'Enjoyed?'

I responded with enthusiasm, 'A lot.'

After an extended, somewhat uneasy pause, Vikrant gathered his thoughts and asked, 'Can I ask you something?'

'Of course,' I replied, welcoming the conversation.

He ventured further, 'Are you dating anyone?'

Without hesitation, I replied, 'No.'

For reasons known only to him, he heaved a sigh and responded with a resigned, 'Okay.'

Curiosity aroused, he delved deeper, asking, 'So, any ex?'

I acknowledged, 'Yes, I did have one.'

Vikrant's interest was piqued, and he probed, 'Oh, what happened?'

I began recounting the story of my past relationship.

'I agreed to his proposal when I was 16 years old. His name is Shiv. He is eight years my senior. However, I believed that he truly loved me and would never abandon me. And when you genuinely love someone, age differences don't matter. I was devoted to him. He was obviously my first love, so I had to ask,'

'Then?'

'Our relationship lasted three years. The situation was excellent. We were both content. But eventually, disagreements emerged. First, we used to talk nonstop. Then we agreed to have a set time for speaking. Then once every two days. Next, once per week. Then, he totally stopped paying attention to me. Yes. I was mistaken when I initially assumed that it was because of his education.

'I made the decision to surprise him one day by going to his house. But it was me who was taken by surprise. Shiv and his new girlfriend opened the door just as I was about to ring the doorbell. She held his hand as they both grinned without acknowledging my presence. That's when I realised the reality.'

'Then?'

'Nothing; this concludes our tale. They are now happily married and leading fulfilling lives,' I said.

'Okay,' he responded.

I added, 'But you know what, I really loved him.'

He merely retorted, 'Hmm.'

I asked myself, 'Idiot, was there any need to say that?'

Suddenly, I continued to hold onto his shoulders. I accidentally said, 'Hey, don't worry, I am still a virgin.'

'What are you saying, idiot?' Once more, my inner voice asks, 'Do you have any idea of it?'

Vikrant's blue irises were protruding. He did not anticipate hearing that from me.

Oh, dear.

He gave me a startled glance for a short while. Then, though, hilarity broke out in full force. I followed him in.

Curiosity got the better of me, and I couldn't resist asking, 'Do you have any girlfriends?' Inwardly, I hoped for a "no."

My heart leaped with joy when Vikrant answered in the affirmative, 'No.'

I sighed in relief.

I couldn't help but probe further, 'Any ex?'

To my surprise, Vikrant responded, 'I had one,' and at that moment, it felt like my heart shattered into a million pieces.

Desiring to know more, I asked, 'What happened then?'

Vikrant began to share his past, 'Kriti is her name. She didn't want me to enlist in the Indian Army.'

'What?' I was taken aback by this revelation.

Vikrant continued, 'Yes. She gave me an ultimatum. It was either the Army or her. Love or my dream.'

'And you chose your dream, right?' I inquired.

With a thoughtful 'Hmm,' Vikrant confirmed his choice.

'I'm still a virgin, though,' he continued. Now, it was my irises that bulged. Another fit of laughter broke out, but this time it was coming from me.

'And could you please do me a favour?' he enquired.

'What?'

'Stop constantly focusing on my butts. You know, it is pretty humiliating.'

Oh shit, he noticed it.

I was so humiliated that I said, 'Aaa.. sorry.'

He exclaimed, 'Ha ha ha.' I followed suit.

I had many of questions swirling in my mind. What was it that made Vikrant and me different? Why did he rush to my aid when I was in danger? Why did he always come to rescue me? Was he just a good guy, or was there something more? And why did I feel so comfortable when we talked? Was it just a friendship, or was it something deeper?

After that day, life had kept us both busy. I had a mountain of tasks to tackle, which meant I had to put in extra hours at work. When I finally got back to my apartment, I'd collapse into bed, sometimes even skipping dinner. But the moment I talked to Vikrant, all my fatigue seemed to vanish.

❑

CHAPTER 7

Loves Awakening

February 2016, Newtown, Kolkata

'Can we meet this evening? It's crucial,' I texted Vikrant.

'Certainly,' he answered.

'Where? In Victoria Garden?'

He responded with a palms up, 'Done.'

Four months had elapsed. Vikrant and I found our friendship growing stronger and deeper. We supported each other through life's challenges, celebrating victories and sharing moments of joy. Our bond became unbreakable, defying the tests of time and circumstance.

But beneath the surface of our friendship, something was changing, though we didn't speak of it openly. In the stolen glances, the gentle touches, and the warmth of our companionship, I began to feel a connection that transcended friendship. Vikrant's laughter became music to my soul, his smile lit up my world, and his presence filled my heart with warmth.

I noticed the way his eyes sparkled when he spoke about his dreams, and how his touch sent shivers down my spine. Vikrant, too, began to see me differently. My unwavering steady support, my kind heart, and my infectious laughter had woven their way into his being. He realized he had fallen in love with the girl who had been his shield, his confidante, and his best friend.

Yet, we both hesitated to acknowledge these newfound feelings. We feared that moving from friendship to romance might jeopardize the trust and understanding we had built over time. Our hearts silently longed for each other, our souls yearning for a love that went beyond friendship. We were caught in a delicate dance, afraid to disrupt the harmony we had nurtured.

Eventually, I decided it was time to find answers. Love has a unique way of making you see your partner as someone truly special. You focus on their strengths, cherish the small precious moments, and feel emotions like possessiveness, jealousy, and a fear of losing them. Deep love brings empathy, the ability to feel their pain as your own, and a burning desire to do anything for them.

When you are deeply in love, your relationship transforms with emotional and physical intimacy, a passionate connection, and a thirst to know everything about each other. Vikrant and I were on the verge of discovering this profound love, but we had to overcome our hesitations and fears to embrace what our hearts truly desired.

'You can't live without Vikrant because you love him. Accept it,' advised my inner voice.

But what would he say in response? I had two ailments:

1. If he responds 'yes,' I'll jump up and down and hug him tightly all day.

2. If he rejects me, I will never think of it ever again.

…

'Hey, Good evening.' I sat next to him. He responded by wishing me good evening.

'So Prana, why did you want to meet me today?' he asked, which really made me feel uncomfortable. I was already anxious, and now I was even more anxious.

I mustered all my resolve and said, 'I just want to tell you something.'

'Let's go,' he said.

'Actually,' I said, unable to speak. I lost my entire script.

'What's the matter, Prano?' he enquired. My stomach fluttered like a butterfly.

'Vikrant I think.. I think. I feel as if I love you.'

Long periods of stillness.

'Are you serious?' he asked, breaking the ice.

'Indeed, Vikrant. I love you.' I said, 'You are the one I want to share the rest of my life with.'

I've finished now. Nothing further. It could be regarded as the worst proposal ever. But folks, remember that he is not an average person. A Para Commando, and my best friend, he is. Consequently, you could understand why I was anxious.

He said, 'Prano, I love you too,' which allowed joy to enter my heart. 'But,' he continued.

'But what?' I questioned. He got up.

'I care deeply for you, Prana. I don't want to see you suffer in any way. Being the spouse of a military person is far from simple. It completely changes your life. There won't be any consistency in our lives if we get married. I've mentioned this before, but it's important that you understand. My duty often involves dangerous tasks, and I can't predict how much time I'll be able to spend with you.'

The gravity of his words hung in the air. Vikrant tried to protect me from the heartache and uncertainty that military life could bring. His love for me was evident, but he also understood the immense challenges we would face if we chose to be together. It was a difficult decision, and the reality of it was far from the romantic fairy tales we might have imagined.

He turned to face me, his eyes filled with concern. 'Pranali, this isn't a fairy tale. It's the reality of military life. My father, Captain Vikram Shergil, was a former army commander. I saw how my mother endured during his missions. She would stay up all night, sometimes going without eating. She cried endlessly. I don't want you to go through that, Prana. What if I go on a mission and never come back? What if....,' I felt necessary to shut his mouth. So I sealed his lips with mine. Yes, you were correct to guess.

Our first kiss.

It only lasted for four to five seconds. But a first kiss is a first kiss. I was happier than ever as a result.

'I completely understand if you need some time to think about this. I just couldn't hold back my feelings any longer. Vikrant, you've always been by my side, supporting and understanding me like no one else ever has. You've been my best friend, and now, I want to take our relationship to the next level. I want to be more than just a friend; I want to be your partner, the one you confide in, and the person who loves you with all my heart.'

'I need some time to sort through my own feelings. Can you give me that?' asked Vikrant. I nodded, a small smile gracing my lips.

'Of course, Vikrant. Take all the time you need. Just know that whatever you decide, our friendship will always be the base of our relationship. I'm here for you, no matter what.'

❑

CHAPTER 8

Pranali, Para Commando's Girlfriend

March 2016, Newtown, Kolkata

Days turned into weeks as Vikrant wrestled with his emotions. He really valued our friendship, and thinking about taking it to a romantic level excited and scared him at the same time. He spent a lot of time thinking about the moments we'd shared, the laughter, and how we'd always been there for each other.

I understood what was going on in Vikrant's mind. Love isn't something you rush into. It takes time, and sometimes, it's a bit scary. I respected his need for time and space to figure things out. During this waiting period, I focused on keeping our friendship strong, making sure it didn't change.

One evening, we sat together in our favourite spot, at Victoria Garden. The atmosphere was charged with a mix of excitement and a touch of nervousness. The weather was gloomy, and it looked like heavy rain was on the way. Vikrant was already there when I arrived, wearing a stylish brown leather overcoat. Finally, he broke the silence that hung between us.

'Pranali, these past weeks have given me a chance to truly understand my feelings,' he began, his voice steady but tinged with vulnerability. 'And I've realized that my heart longs for you too. The love I feel for you goes beyond friendship. It's deep, intense, and undeniable.' A rush of joy and relief washed over me as I listened to his words. A wide smile spread across my face, illuminating the room.

'Vikrant, I can't tell you how happy I am to hear that. My heart has been waiting for this moment, hoping that our love would find its way.'

Vikrant took my hands in his. 'Pranali, you are everything I've ever wanted and more. You've been my guiding light, my pillar of strength, and my source of inspiration. I can't imagine my life without you.'

Suddenly, raindrops began to fall from the sky. Vikrant pointed to a nearby tree, signaling for us to take shelter. We dashed over and huddled beneath its branches just as the rain intensified, becoming a heavy downpour. The icy raindrops brushed against my skin, causing me to shiver uncontrollably.

Vikrant quickly took off his jacket and draped it over my shoulders, trying to shield me from the biting cold. But I knew that his embrace was the warmest thing in the world. I hugged him tightly in return, feeling the strength of his arms around me. I could sense his warmth, and the scent of his neck filled my senses. In that moment, it felt like the world around us was fading away, and all that existed was the profound connection between Vikrant and me.

He had a warm scent. He had icy cheeks. My pulse began to beat very quickly and abnormally. It seemed as though it would simply emerge from my thoracic cage and I would pass away instantly. His eyes were closed, which caught my attention, and I immediately forgot myself in the fragrance. I kissed him. I kissed him because I was out of it.

Gosh!

It was merely a kiss. Nothing, not even a smooch. It did, however, go on for at least 20 minutes.

I finally became PARA COMMANDO's girlfriend. I began to daydream about the future. Future, filled with joy and contentment. For me, it was just like a fairy tale.

…

I remember that serious moment when I decided to share the truth about my relationship with Vikrant with my parents. It was a decision driven by my desire for honesty and transparency, even if the outcome was uncertain. I picked up the phone, my heart pounding, and dialed their number.

As I began to speak, explaining the depth of my feelings for Vikrant, my mother listened intently, her voice a mix of understanding and concern. She wanted me to be happy, but she also worried about the challenges our relationship might face, given Vikrant's military service.

My father, on the other hand, remained silent throughout the conversation. His lack of response was palpable, and I could sense the weight of his thoughts. It was as if he had chosen not to engage in the conversation, leaving me with an uneasy sense of uncertainty.

In the days that followed, our love story blossomed, touching the lives of those around us. Our bond became an example of how friendship could be the foundation for a love that transcended expectations. And as we stood hand in hand, facing the world together, Vikrant and I knew that our love, fortified by the strength of our friendship, would stand the test of time. With hearts full of gratitude and a future brimming with endless possibilities, we embraced the beauty of our love story, knowing that our journey had only just begun. Now the true story will begin. The love story. Story of suffering. A tale about commitment. And a tale of sacrifices.

❑

Part B

The Narration was Interrupted by Dr. Sameer's Phone Ringtone...

CHAPTER 9

I Will Wait for Him

October 2018, Andheri East, Mumbai

Dr. Sameer arched an eyebrow while looking at his phone.

'I'm sorry, Pranali, but I have to take this call.'

Pranali responded, 'Yes sure, go ahead.'

After picking up his phone, Dr. Sameer moved a short distance away from her. Pranali observed that while their conversation was going on, they had arrived from a great distance. Finding someone with whom she could discuss her background gave her a sense of relief. Dr. Sameer approached her and took a position in front of her.

'Pranali, I'm really sorry, but I have to go to the hospital. One of my patients in the ICU is in pretty bad shape, and he needs me there.'

Pranali responded, 'Ohh... then you must leave as soon as possible.'

'Yes. However, I'll listen to the entire earlier story without a doubt.'

'Yes, absolutely,' Pranali replied with a smile.

Dr. Sameer remarked, looking for his car key in his pocket, 'You wait here and I'll bring my car.'

'No. You need to get out of here as quickly as possible. So just go away right now. I'm going home alone.'

'Sure?'

'Yes. Now depart.'

'All right, then,' Dr. Sameer remarked, 'See you,' and then he left.

Pranali reserved a taxi. She was forced to stay there till it arrived. Pranali spotted one or two people whose faces were concealed by black hoodies. She stood up and looked at their shifting shapes in confusion.

Are they thieves?

As Pranali walked, lost in her thoughts, someone suddenly collided with her from behind. It was an unexpected jolt that nearly sent her tumbling forward. But in that very moment, strong arms reached out and caught her, preventing her from falling to the ground.

Pranali's heart raced as she realized that the person who had caught her was wearing the same black hoodie as the mysterious individuals she had seen earlier, the ones who had raised her suspicions. Their face remained hidden in the shadows, but a few intriguing details caught her attention.

Beneath the hood, she glimpsed a pair of striking blue eyes that seemed oddly familiar. It was a gaze she couldn't forget, even if she tried. The touch of the person's hands against her skin resonated with a sense of recognition, like an old friend or a loved one she hadn't seen in a long time.

As she steadied herself in the arms of this hooded figure, Pranali couldn't help but notice the strong and familiar frame that held her. It was a body she knew well, and the scent that enveloped her was undeniably recognizable.

In that fleeting moment, Pranali's mind raced with questions and possibilities. Who was this person hidden beneath the hoodie, and why did they seem so strangely familiar? The encounter left her both bewildered and intrigued, setting the stage for a mystery that was yet to unfold in her life.

Is it "HIM"?

Pranali became more perplexed as she noticed tears forming in the hooded figure's eyes. Hooded finger left her and fled as soon as she regained her equilibrium.

Who was he? Everything about him—his touch, his eyes, his scent—felt comfortable. Was he really him? What on earth is he doing in Mumbai? What made him run? If it was indeed him, why did he flee even after plainly seeing my face? No. It must be a mistake on my part, I believe. He couldn't be the one. He wouldn't have treated me like a stranger if he really was him. The most crucial thing is that he would be in Kashmir rather than Mumbai. I would have let you know when he came back.

The taxi has arrived. She entered it while contemplating the hooded person she had just crashed into.

...

Pranali's father, Pranav was waiting for her in the living room as she returned home. Pranav approached her as soon as she arrived and began asking about her visit with Dr. Sameer. Anjali, Pranali's mother, asked him to wait till she was feeling better before telling him.

Pranali entered the living room after getting up.

'How did your meeting with Dr. Sameer go, Pranali?' As soon as she had rested on the couch, Pranav asked.

'I wanted to discuss that with you, dad. It didn't go as planned,' answered Pranali. Anjali entered the living room and sat besides Pranav.

'What happened Prana? Sameer is a genuinely nice person. He appears to be really interested in you.' Pranav tried to persuade her by saying, 'I think he would make a wonderful husband.'

'I am confident in his goodness. Dad, but I had to be open with him throughout our meeting. I informed him of Vikrant. I expressed to him my affection for Vikrant. And I expressed my eagerness to see him.'

'We don't even know if Vikrant is still alive,' Pranav added, sighing to Pranali, 'He had been absent for several months.'

'I know that, Dad, but he has my heart,' she said. 'Even if Sameer seems like a perfect match on paper, I can't just move on with someone else.' Pranav became irritated while listening to this. Anjali simply listened in silence.

'Pranali, things changed, and sometimes we had to make tough decisions. You can't hold out hope that someone might come along.'

Pranali interrupted and said, 'Dad Although it's difficult to take, I promised Vikrant that I would wait for him, and I can't go back on that commitment, not even for someone as great as Sameer.' Pranav and Anjali both felt a brief hush.

'We only want the best for you, Pranali. We believed that Dr. Sameer could offer you a safe and happy future, but if Vikrant is your heart's desire, we won't force you into something you don't want,' stated Anjali.

Pranav gently replied, 'I may not agree with your decision, but I respect it Prana,' while keeping his hand on Pranali's shoulders. 'Whatever path you pick, just promise me that you will be careful and take care of yourself.' Pranali was able to sense compassion and love in her father's eyes.

'I promise, dad,' Pranali said as she grabbed Pranav's hand in hers. 'And I'll always be appreciative of your support and love. Even though accepting my decisions is difficult.'

'That's my child. Prana, I want you to be happy. regardless of where life leads you.' Pranali nodded before walking into her room.

Pranali lay on the bed, leaving her phone on the table, as she contemplated her future and looked at the sealing. Not that waiting for Vikrant is worthwhile or not, but she has been jobless for months. She left her work without giving it a second thought when she learned that Vikrant had gone MIA. She made the decision to wait till Vikrant returns with his family. But after being persuaded by both families to continue living, she went back to Mumbai, where she was born. She was now in dire need of a job. Pranali stood up and began to observe the constellations that decorated the night sky.

When Anjali entered Pranali's room, she discovered her daughter sitting by the window, lost in concentration, admiring the constellations in the night sky. She could clearly see the worry that had been engraved on Pranali's face ever since her Para commando boyfriend, Major Vikrant, vanished in combat.

Anjali walked over to Pranali and sat down next to her with a soft grin on her face. She was aware of the depth of her daughter's suffering and the persistent presence of Vikrant's need. Pranali's unshakeable devotion to her love had always been something Anjali admired, but she also wanted her daughter to be happy.

'Pranali,' Anjali began softly, 'I respect your decision to wait for Vikrant. Your love for him is deep and genuine, and I've seen the strength it gives you. But, my dear, I want you to remember something crucial – your happiness matters just as much.'

Pranali turned to her mother, her eyes glistening with unshed tears. 'I know, Mom. It's just that I can't imagine being happy with anyone else. Vikrant means everything to me.'

Anjali placed a reassuring hand on Pranali's shoulder. 'I understand, sweetheart. Vikrant is a remarkable man, and your love is a testament to that. But life can be unpredictable, and sometimes it takes us down unexpected paths. I want you to be open to the possibility of happiness, even if it's not the path you initially envisioned.'

Pranali nodded, her heart heavy with conflicting emotions. 'I'll try, Mom, but it's so hard. Vikrant is the love of my life, and I can't imagine loving anyone else.'

Anjali leaned in, offering her daughter a comforting embrace. 'I know, dear. But remember, happiness can take many forms. It might not replace the love you have for Vikrant, but it can complement it. Don't close yourself off to life's possibilities.'

Pranali sighed, resting her head on her mother's shoulder. 'I'll keep that in mind, Mom. It's just that I miss him so much, and the uncertainty is hard to bear.'

Anjali stroked Pranali's hair gently. 'I know, my love. We all miss Vikrant, and we pray for his safe return every day. But while you wait, don't forget to live your life. Pursue your dreams, find moments of joy, and surround yourself with love and support. Vikrant would want that for you.'

Pranali wiped away a tear and smiled weakly. 'You're right, Mom. I'll try to find happiness in the small moments, even as I hold onto hope for Vikrant's return.'

Anjali hugged her daughter tightly. 'That's my girl. You're strong, and your love for Vikrant is beautiful. Just remember that your happiness matters, too. We'll get through this together.'

In that quiet moment, mother and daughter shared an understanding that went beyond words. Anjali would always support Pranali's unwavering love for Vikrant, but she also hoped that her daughter would find happiness, whether it was in waiting or in embracing new opportunities. Their love would guide them through the uncertainty, and together they would face whatever the future held.

Pranali's phone rang as soon as Anjali left the room. As soon as she took it up, "Mr. Khanna" began to flash on the screen. The call reached her.

'Hello, sir'.

'Hello. How are you today, Pranali?'

'I'm fine, sir. How about you?'

'I'm okay, too. Look Pranali, Sonal informed me what had happened with you,' Mr. Khanna continued, 'We have a job vacancy, which is why I phoned you. Therefore, you can re-join us if you need the position.'

Pranali grew ecstatic. She agreed to his offer and informed him that she would start working for the company in seven days. That pleased Mr. Khanna. Pranali wanted to tell her parents this wonderful news right away, but she ultimately decided to wait till the following morning.

...

'Dad, I want to tell you something'

Pranali sat infront of her dad on a chair. He was reading a newspaper. Anjali was right their watching news channel.

'What Prana?'

News reporter from the TV channel said, 'In a shocking turn of events, tragedy struck the city of Mumbai on a quiet evening when Mr. Ramesh Kumar, a businessman from Delhi and a Russian businessman, Mr. Igor Petrov were brutally killed during their meeting. The incident unfolded in the bustling suburb of Andheri, sending shockwaves throughout the nation.

'The meeting between the two, shrouded in secrecy, had taken place at the secret place for security reasons in the heart of Andheri, known for its exquisite cuisine and discretion.

'Peoples recount that several individuals dressed in black hoodies, their faces concealed, exited from the same place where gunshot sounds were heard.

'The identity of the assailants remains a mystery, and investigators are working tirelessly to unravel the intricate web of events leading up to this gruesome crime. The motive behind this brazen attack is yet unknown, and speculation abounds, from political vendettas to international intrigue.

'The Andheri Police Department swiftly cordoned off the crime scene, launching a thorough investigation into the murders. The entire area was placed under heightened security, and all possible leads are being pursued with utmost diligence. Close-circuit cameras in the vicinity are being reviewed to identify the suspects.'

Hearing the news left everyone in the living room speechless. Pranali became submerged in thinking. She was familiar with the person shown on camera by the CCTV system. They were the same people she had seen the previous evening. Additionally, one of them crashed into her.

He wasn't Vikrant, no. Never would Vikrant do it.

Pranav shouted, 'Oh god, how ruthless some people can be.'

'When will all this end?' asked Anjali.

Pranav asked her, 'What were you thinking about Prana?' to get her attention.

'Dad, I received a call from Mr. Khanna last night.' 'Mr. Khanna? Means your previous boss? Pranav questioned.

'Yes. He invited me back and gave me a job.

'What? That's very wonderful news,' Pranav exclaimed.

'Yes. He said if I want, then I can rejoin the company.' Anjali and Pranav were more joyful than ever.

'That's fantastic. What then did you decide?

'I'm going back to the company. He gave me a week. So I suppose I ought to leave after two days.'

'Good. Now put the past behind you and concentrate only on the future,' Pranav said.

When Pranali reached her bedroom, she dialled Dr. Sameer's number.

'How are you today?' Sameer enquired.

'Great. You?'

'I'm fine, too.'

'I had something I wanted to tell you. In reality, I am going to Kolkata to re-join my previous company.'

'That is truly wonderful news, Pranali. Congratulations,' exclaimed Dr. Sameer. 'It means we have to meet tonight,' he continued.

'Well, of course. But why?'

'Because you haven't brought your story to a close.' Remember?'

'Ahh.. yes'

'I'll see you at 5pm, and then we'll head to Choupatty Beach.'

'Choupatty beach?'

'Yes. Any issues?

Never at all.

'Then be ready.'

'Sure.'

…

Pranali and Dr. Sameer arrived at Choupatty Beach as the sun dipped below the horizon, ushering in the enchanting beauty of the ocean at night. The scene before them was nothing short of mesmerizing.

The beach, now bathed in the soft, silvery light of the moon, stretched out like a tranquil canvas. The gentle waves lapped at the shore, creating a soothing symphony that seemed to harmonize with the beating of their hearts. The sands glistened under the moonlight, resembling a shimmering carpet laid out beneath a star-studded sky.

As they walked closer to the water's edge, the ocean revealed its secrets. The waves, kissed by the silvery moonlight, sparkled like a million tiny diamonds, creating a path of ethereal illumination that extended into the endless expanse of the sea. Each wave brought with it a sense of calm and wonder, as if the ocean itself held the mysteries of the universe within its depths.

Pranali and Dr. Sameer found a quiet spot, where they could sit and absorb the beauty of the night. They watched as the moonlight danced upon the water's surface, creating a pathway to the horizon. The scent of the salty sea air and the soft caress of the gentle breeze added to the sensory delight of the moment.

Dr. Sameer, captivated by the scene, turned to Pranali and said, 'This is truly magical, isn't it?'

Pranali smiled, her eyes reflecting the moonlight, and replied, 'It's moments like these that remind us of the immense beauty of the world. Nature has a way of bringing peace and wonder into our lives.'

'So, can we proceed?' Dr. Sameer asked excitedly.

'Yes'

PRANALI BEGAN THE NARRATION…

❑

CHAPTER 10

Love in the Air

August 2016, Newtown Kolkata

Six months elapsed. In those six months with Vikrant, our love had been tested in ways I could have never imagined. Loneliness and depression had become unwelcome guests in our lives, threatening to overshadow the love we held for each other. But despite the trials, we found our way out of the darkness.

Four long, agonizing days had slipped by without a single word from Vikrant, and it felt like an eternity. Frustration had been building within me, like a pressure cooker on the verge of exploding. My phone had become a constant companion, an instrument of torment that I couldn't put down, hoping against hope for a message or a missed call that never came.

I had sent him texts, one after the other, each carrying a mix of concern and longing, but they had all vanished into the abyss of his silence. It was driving me mad, this relentless uncertainty that had taken residence in my mind. I replayed our last conversation over and over, desperately searching for clues to explain this sudden disconnect.

Finally, my call connected, and his voice came through the phone. 'Vikrant,' I began, my voice tentative, 'I feel like we don't spend as much time together as we used to. Is everything fine?'

Vikrant, his mood already soured by a difficult day, had reacted defensively. 'Pranali, you don't understand what it's like out there. I have responsibilities, and it's not always easy to make time.'

'I'm just asking for a little more of your time, Vikrant,' I implored, my voice trembling with emotion.

But he snapped back, his frustration palpable, and abruptly disconnected the call. I was left in disbelief. How dare he speak to me like that?

The uncertainty continued to gnaw at my thoughts, and in my frustration, I made a decision. I wouldn't be the one to break the silence; it was up to him to reach out first. The ball was in his court.

The next evening, my phone rang, displaying Vikrant's name on the screen. Anger still smouldered within me, so I ignored the call. He tried calling again, and I disconnected once more. This happened several times, and with each call, my frustration grew. By the sixth attempt, someone rang my doorbell, interrupting the phone's insistent ringing.

I chose to ignore the call again and went to answer the door. To my utter surprise, there stood Vikrant, dressed in black trousers and a white t-shirt. He called out to me, and I couldn't help but think he was acting a bit crazily.

'May I come in, madam?' he asked, but I responded with a glare, saying nothing. He entered, closing the door behind him, and followed me to the couch, where he took a seat beside me.

'Still angry, ma'am?' he inquired, placing his hand on mine.

I pulled my hand away and crossed my arms over my chest. 'No. Who am I to be angry with you?'

'Sorry, babes,' he said, but my silence persisted. I was enjoying my little act.

Then he mentioned he had something for me and began searching his pocket. He revealed a pair of jasmine-shaped jhumkaas, my favourite. My heart leaped with happiness, and I had already forgiven him for his behaviour, but I wanted to keep him on his toes a bit longer.

So, with a typical girl's drama, I responded, 'Thank you,' with an expressionless face, watching as his gaze fell.

'Do you like it?' he asked, his eyes hopeful.

'Hmm,' I replied, keeping up the act.

'Do you want Gillette guard?' he asked, baffling me.

'Why?' I asked in confusion.

'Shave with Gillette guard and say whatever you want,' he said, laughing. However, his laughter died down as he received no response from me.

'That was a very unfunny joke,' I said irritably, leaning back on the couch, which inadvertently caused my t-shirt to ride up, revealing my navel.

Vikrant's eyes widened as he fixed his gaze on my navel. I quickly covered it when I noticed, and he averted his gaze, embarrassed. A soft laugh escaped me.

'I want something to eat,' he added, shifting the conversation.

I walked towards kitchen unknowing that he was following me. When I reached the door, he grabbed me from back and rested his right arm around my waist. I closed my eyes, because it was the first time he touched me their.

'When I said I want to eat something. I meant you,' he whispered in my ears and kissed the back of my neck. He pinched on my navel.

'I haven't forgiven you yet.' I whispered still my eyes closed.

He turned me. When I faced him, he pulled my hair back and kissed my neck. His tongue glided on my neck.

Heaven.

'Now?' he asked.

'No,' I replied.

He picked me up and headed towards the bedroom. He dropped me on the bed and started scanning my whole body with his dark blue eyes. He started opening the button of his shirt, his gaze still fixed on me. He undressed himself and started to head towards me slowly. Like a hungry lion.

He kept his right hand on my cheeks and started kissing me. First my forehead, then temples, then eyes, cheeks, jaw and chin.

'Is this enough?'

'Not at all'.

He grinned like a devil and rested his lips over me gently. Slowly he accelerated and started kissing me passionately. His tongue was inside my mouth, exploring every corner of my mouth. I closed my eyes tightly and grabbed his naked back. Slowly he started to kiss my neck. His tongue was doing magic.

He grabbed my shirt and said, 'This thing… is irritating me.'

'Then remove it,' I said with a sigh. He removed my shirt and fixed his gaze on my navel. His mouth reached it and started kissing it mercilessly. He was kissing it, biting it, sucking it and doing everything he could.

'Huh,' I groaned and grabbed his hair.

'Oh god Prana. You are like a drug. I want to devour you completely.'

'Then eat me,' I said, my eyes still closed.

When he had finished, he brought his face near me.

'Is this enough?'

‘Enough for now. But I want more after our marriage,’ I said. He grinned.

He rested his head on my naked bosom.

Not completely naked.

I started playing with his hair.

‘Prana,’ Vikrant’s voice called out to me.

I responded with a questioning ‘Um?’

‘Have you planned anything about our future?’ he asked with innocence in his eyes.

I pondered for a moment before admitting, ‘Not yet.’

He suggested, ‘Then let’s plan it,’ and locked his gaze with mine, resting his chin on my chest. His presence was comforting.

‘After our marriage, we will settle in Kolkata, so that you can continue your job,’ he shared.

Curious, I inquired about his own plans, ‘What have you decided to do after your retirement?’

Vikrant’s face lit up as he replied, ‘I am thinking of working as a teacher in the army training academy. I want to help the youngsters fulfil their dream of joining the Indian army.’

I smiled warmly at his idea. ‘That’s a really great idea,’ I acknowledged, appreciating his dedication.

The conversation shifted to a lighter note as he playfully moved his attention lower, reaching my stomach, which had turned a delightful shade of red due to his earlier affections.

‘Hey, how many babies do you want?’ he asked, his tone still innocent.

I considered for a moment before responding, ‘Um... 1.’

With a twinkle in his eye, Vikrant inquired further, ‘A boy or a girl?’

I playfully replied, ‘A boy.’

He looked at me and kissed my stomach. 'But I want a girl,' he countered, disagreeing with my choice.

Curious, I questioned, 'Why?'

His answer was filled with warmth, 'Because I heard that daughters are close to their father.'

I chuckled, 'Oh really?'

With affection in his eyes, he rested his head on my navel, his longing evident as he said, 'I am eagerly waiting for that day, Prana.'

Then, his tone grew sombre, and he broached a difficult topic. 'But what if anything happens to…' I quickly hushed him, placing my hand over his mouth.

Exasperated, I implored, 'How many times do I have to tell you? Please don't talk about such grim things.'

He removed my hand gently and requested, 'Please promise me one thing.'

I asked, 'What?'

'If something happens to me,' he began solemnly, 'You will carry on. If something happens to me before our marriage, you will forget me and marry a nice guy. If something happens to me after our marriage, then also you will consider a second marriage.'

Tears welled up in my eyes as frustration and sadness intertwined. 'Why are you talking about such heart-breaking possibilities?' I asked, my voice laden with frustration.

Vikrant reminded me of the harsh realities of his profession. 'Prana, I told you before. Our lives are not certain. We face death matches every day. We have to perform dangerous missions in extreme situations.'

I relented, saying, 'Okay, I will promise you.'

He looked at me, his eyes searching mine for sincerity.

I declared firmly, 'I promise you that I will wait for you. When you are at the army HQ, I will wait for you. When you are on your postings, I will wait for you. When you are on your missions, I will wait for you. And even if you never return, I will wait for you. If I have to wait for six lifetimes to be reunited with you in the seventh, then I will wait for you.'

Tears from Vikrant's eyes fell on my chest, a rare display of vulnerability from a strong soldier. It was the first time I had witnessed tears in his eyes, a sight that didn't quite suit him.

He kissed me passionately, his words unspoken but filled with the depth of his love. 'I love you so much, Prana,' he whispered as his lips met mine.

My heart swelled with love as I responded, 'I love you too, Vikrant,' and hugged him tightly, cherishing the warmth of our embrace.

We kissed throughout the night, savouring each moment of our profound connection.

❑

CHAPTER 11

The Twist of Fate

August 2016, Newtown Kolkata

I gazed out at the Kolkata skyline, a sense of unease settling in my chest. My father's unexpected arrival had left me with a heavy heart, and I couldn't help but feel that something was amiss. His usual cheerful demeanour had been replaced by an unspoken tension, and it was clear that there was more to his visit than met the eye. He had mentioned coming to meet me, but it felt as if there was a storm brewing within him, something he wasn't sharing.

In just a day, he left just as suddenly as he had arrived, leaving me bewildered and confused. What puzzled me even more was that he hadn't even met Vikrant, the love of my life, whom I had hoped he would come to know.

The unanswered questions swirled in my mind, intensifying the whirlwind of emotions that had taken hold of me. I couldn't get over the feeling that his visit had held a deeper purpose, one that remained shrouded in mystery. As I stood there, staring at the cityscape, I couldn't help but wonder about the secrets my father had carried with him and the impact they might have on the path ahead.

...

The following day, as I reached for my phone, a pang of dread washed over me. A message from Vikrant, my beloved, awaited my gaze. With trembling hands, I opened the text, and my world shattered into a thousand fragmented pieces.

The words on the screen formed a breakup letter, each sentence piercing my heart like shards of glass.

"I have spent many sleepless nights trying to find the right words to say, but I fear there is no easy way to express what I am about to write. Our journey together has been filled with beautiful moments and cherished memories, but I have reached a point where I believe it is best for us to part ways.

I wish I could provide a clear and definitive reason for my decision, but the truth is that my feelings have become clouded and uncertain. It pains me to admit this, but I have found myself questioning the depth of my love for you. It would be unfair to continue our relationship when my heart is no longer fully committed. Please understand that this decision has not come easily. I have wrestled with my emotions, hoping that clarity would emerge, but the doubts persist. I believe it is only fair to both of us to seek a path that allows us to find happiness and fulfilment, even if it means doing so separately.

With a heavy heart, I say goodbye, Pranali. May life's blessings be yours, and may you find the love and happiness that you truly deserve."

I read the message over and over, hoping to find some hidden meaning, some reason behind this sudden demand for a breakup. My mind raced, trying to make sense of what had gone wrong, but there were no answers, only uncertainty.

Tears blurred my phone screen as I struggled to grasp the weight of his words. It felt like a thousand knives had pierced my heart, leaving an unbearable ache.

I tried to call him, text him, but he was not replying to any of it.

Confusion overwhelmed me. How could everything we shared, all our promises and dreams, crumble so easily? I clung to memories of our laughter and the warmth of his touch, but it all felt like a cruel joke, slipping away. Doubts crept in, whispering that I wasn't enough.

I questioned every moment, seeking a sign or clue to unravel this mystery. But there was nothing, only silence and unanswered questions. Anguish gripped me, tearing through my facade of strength.

I felt lost, with a future that once seemed so clear now distant and unattainable. Clutching my phone, I allowed myself to grieve, to mourn the loss. Healing wouldn't come easy; the wound was deep.

Days turned into nights, and I found myself descending into a pit of darkness. My heart ached with a profound emptiness, and each passing moment felt like a lifetime of sorrow. Depression engulfed me, casting a shadow over even the simplest joys of life. The world seemed colourless, devoid of the vibrant hues that once illuminated my existence. But amidst the abyss of my despair, a flicker of determination ignited within me. I couldn't bear the thought of losing Vikrant without an explanation. I yearned for closure, for a chance to understand why our love had been torn asunder.

...

Weeks turned into a painful and seemingly endless stretch of time, and I found myself unable to fully recover from the emotional impact of Vikrant's abrupt breakup letter. The days felt heavy, filled with longing and unanswered questions. It was a period of deep reflection and soul-searching, as I grappled with the ache of lost love and the haunting uncertainty of our future.

One day, as I was lost in thought, my phone rang, jolting me back to reality. I glanced at the caller ID and saw that it was my father calling. His name on the screen brought a mix of anticipation and anxiety.

'Pranali,' he began, 'I need you to take some time off from your job and come back to Mumbai for a few days.' His voice, usually warm and reassuring, carried a sense of urgency that immediately caught my attention.

The request struck me as odd and left me with a flurry of questions. Why the sudden urgency? What could be so important that required my immediate presence in Mumbai? My mind raced with possibilities, none of which seemed to fit the usual rhythm of our family's life.

I asked my father for more details, but he remained somewhat cryptic, only stating that there were matters that needed to be discussed in person. His tone carried a weight that left me feeling a mixture of curiosity and apprehension.

As I listened to him, I couldn't help but wonder if this had anything to do with Vikrant or the recent events that had transpired.

'All right, Dad,' I responded with a sigh, 'I'll make arrangements to come to Mumbai as soon as I can. But please, can you at least give me a hint about what's going on?'

It will distract my mind from the thoughts of Vikrant.

There was a brief pause on the other end of the line, and then my father replied, 'I promise I'll explain everything when you're here, Pranali. Just know that it's important.'

With a sense of resignation, I began the process of requesting leave from my job and preparing for my return to Mumbai. I texted Vikrant that I am going to Mumbai. But it too remained unrepelled message just like those hundreds of messages I sent him over the past few weeks.

Why is this happening with me?

My journey from Kolkata to my hometown began with a flight, and it was a mix of excitement and apprehension as I made my way to the airport. I had packed my bags the night before, ensuring that I had everything I needed for my trip to Mumbai, my hometown.

I arrived at the Airport with plenty of time to spare before my flight. The bustling terminal was filled with travellers, each with their own destination in mind. After checking in and going through security, I made my way to the departure gate.

As I settled into my seat on the airplane, I couldn't help but feel a sense of nostalgia. Flying always brought back memories of past journeys, and this one felt especially significant, given the mysterious summons from my father that had prompted my return.

The flight took off, and soon, the city of Kolkata was nothing more than a distant view outside the window. I watched as the landscape below changed from the bustling city to the serene countryside, and eventually, the vast expanse of the Arabian Sea came into view. I dared to close my eyes because I don't wanted to think about Vikrant. It would all bring sadness and nothing more.

As the flight made its descent into the Airport in Mumbai, I felt a mixture of emotions. It was always a heart-warming feeling to return to my hometown, with its familiar sights and sounds. I tried hard to stop myself from informing this to Vikrant, but I couldn't.

Once the plane touched down, I collected my luggage and made my way through the airport. As I stepped out into the arrivals area, I scanned the crowd, looking for my father's familiar face among the waiting passengers. Whatever awaited me in Mumbai, I was determined to face it with resolve and an open heart, prepared to uncover the truth behind the mysterious call that had brought me home.

As I entered my childhood home in Mumbai, the familiar sights and sounds of the place washed over me. It was heartening to be back, but my return was clouded with the mystery of my father's urgent request. My mother, Anjali, was the first to greet me with a warm embrace, her eyes reflecting a mother's love and concern.

'Pranali, it's so good to have you back,' she said, holding me close. 'Your father has been waiting eagerly to see you.'

I smiled at my mother's warmth, feeling a sense of comfort in her presence. 'I've missed you, Mom. Is Dad around?'

She nodded and led me into the living room, where my father, Pranav, was waiting. His expression was a mixture of anticipation and seriousness, and I couldn't help but feel a sense of apprehension as I approached him.

'Pranali,' he began, 'There's someone I'd like you to meet. He's here for dinner tonight.'

My curiosity aroused, I nodded in agreement. 'Of course, Dad. Who's coming over?'

It was then that Dr. Sameer arrived, and I couldn't help but notice the recognition in his eyes as he looked at me. But the truth was, I had never met him before, and his presence left me feeling slightly puzzled.

Dr. Sameer extended his hand and greeted me with a warm smile. 'Pranali, it's a pleasure to finally meet you. I've heard so much about you.'

I shook his hand politely, a bit surprised by the familiarity of his tone. 'It's nice to meet you too.'

As the evening progressed, we engaged in polite conversation, discussing our respective backgrounds and interests. Dr. Sameer was an amiable guest, and I appreciated his efforts to make me feel comfortable.

However, as the evening came to a close and Dr. Sameer departed, my father finally revealed the truth that had been shrouded in secrecy. With a heavy heart, he confessed, 'Pranali, there's something important I need to discuss with you. I want you to seriously consider marrying Dr. Sameer.'

His words hung in the air, leaving me stunned and confused. I couldn't fathom why my father was pushing me towards this decision, especially after the events that had unfolded in Kolkata. My heart ached with the weight of this unexpected request, and I knew that a deeper conversation was inevitable, one that would reveal the motivations behind my father's sudden insistence on my marriage to Dr. Sameer.

As my father, pressed on with his insistence that I seriously consider marrying Dr. Sameer, I felt a wave of frustration and helplessness wash over me. I had returned to Mumbai with a heart heavy with unanswered questions, broken heart, and now, faced with this unexpected demand, my emotions threatened to overwhelm me.

With a deep breath, I mustered the courage to speak my truth. 'Dad, I appreciate your concern and the thought you've put into this. But I can't marry Dr. Sameer, or anyone for that matter, right now. I need to focus on my career, and there is someone else in my life that I love deeply.'

My father's expression hardened, and he shook his head, clearly not pleased with my response. 'Pranali, you can't just throw away your future for a soldier. You know the risks involved in loving someone in the military. It's a life of uncertainty and danger.'

I felt my patience wane as I retorted, 'Dad, you've always taught me to follow my heart and pursue my dreams. Vikrant means everything to me, and I can't imagine a life without him. I'll wait for him, no matter how long it takes.'

The argument between us escalated, neither of us willing to back down from our positions. The tension in the room grew palpable, and I could feel tears welling up in my eyes. Frustrated and hurt, I decided it was best to remove myself from the heated exchange.

I stood up abruptly and made my way to my bedroom, my steps heavy with sorrow. As I closed the door behind me, I couldn't contain the tears any longer. I sat their resting my back on the door grabbing my head, sobbing uncontrollably. The weight of my father's expectations, the pain of our disagreement, and the enduring love I held for Vikrant all overwhelmed me, leaving me sobbing in solitude.

'What am I doing? Fighting for him who don't even trying to reply my messages? Am I doing right or wrong? Is this love or madness?'

In the quiet of my room, I knew that this was a battle I couldn't win through arguments or tears. The path I had chosen, the love I had committed to, was my own to walk. And as I cried on that night, I vowed to continue following my heart, even if it meant defying the wishes of those I loved most.

Despite the lingering tension, I tried to make the most of my time in Mumbai. I spent quality moments with my mother, Anjali, cherishing the warmth and love of our bond. We shared stories, laughter, and even the occasional comforting silence that only family can provide.

Yet, as the days passed, the unspoken sadness and unresolved issues continued to weigh on my heart. My father and I shared polite conversations but carefully avoided the topic that had caused our argument. It was a difficult situation, one that left me torn between my love for Major Vikrant and my desire to mend the strained relationship with my father.

When the fifth day arrived, I knew it was time for me to return to Kolkata. As I packed my bags and prepared to leave, the sadness I had carried with me from our family dispute remained palpable. My mother, sensing my unease, offered me a reassuring hug and whispered, 'Pranali, remember that love and time have a way of healing wounds. Stay strong and true to your heart.'

Her words provided some solace, but the lingering sadness I felt from my father's unspoken disappointment was hard to ignore. I hugged her tightly, knowing that I would miss her deeply and that our family's dynamics had irrevocably changed during this visit.

As I left my childhood home, I couldn't help but feel a sense of melancholy. The relationship with my father had been strained, and the uncertainty of when or if it would ever be repaired weighed heavily on my heart.

...

The journey back to Kolkata was a sombre one. The skies outside mirrored the sadness within, and I found myself reflecting on the complex dynamics of family, love, and the difficult choices we sometimes must make in life.

As I landed in Kolkata, the familiar sights welcomed me back, but the emotional baggage from my visit to Mumbai was not so easily left behind. I knew that my path was fraught with challenges, both in my personal life and my career, but I remained determined to follow my heart, no matter where it led me.

Determined to meet Vikrant one last time and resolve the lingering questions that had haunted me for weeks, I set out for the army headquarters. As I approached the imposing entrance, I couldn't help but feel a sense of trepidation. The security measures were stringent, and entering the premises without official business was not something I had ever attempted before.

The thought of facing Vikrant, the man I loved deeply but who had pushed me away with his heart-wrenching breakup, spurred me forward. I knew that the only way to find answers was to confront him directly.

With each step, my heart raced, and my palms grew clammy. I was aware that I might face resistance from the security personnel, but my determination to see Vikrant one last time fuelled my resolve.

Upon reaching the entrance, I approached the guards and explained my intention to meet someone inside. Their stern expressions softened as I mentioned Vikrant's name, perhaps recognizing the genuine urgency in my voice. After a brief exchange, they allowed me to enter but with strict instructions to proceed directly to the specified location and not to Loiter. One soldier kept following me for the security issues.

As I walked through the corridors of the army headquarters, I couldn't help but feel a mixture of anxiety and anticipation. Each step brought me closer to Vikrant, but it also brought me closer to the moment of truth, where our fate would be decided.

Finally, I reached the designated area and saw Vikrant standing there, his familiar figure framed by the surroundings of the army headquarters.

As I reached him, Vikrant turned to me, his expression a mixture of surprise and frustration. Before he could say anything, I took a step closer and whispered, 'Vikrant, we need to talk.'

Time seemed to stand still as I approached him, the distance between us narrowing with each step. The air was thick with unspoken emotions, and I knew that this meeting held the key to our future.

His eyes narrowed, and his voice carried a stern tone as he responded, 'This is not the time or place, Pranali. We'll talk tonight.'

I felt a pang of disappointment at his refusal to address the issue at that moment, but I respected his need for discretion. With a heavy heart, I nodded in agreement and stepped back, my eyes locked on his as I silently pleaded for answers.

Without further words, I turned and left the army headquarters, my mind racing with questions and emotions. The day seemed to stretch endlessly as I anxiously awaited the call that would hopefully shed light on the truth behind our unexpected break-up.

As I retreated from the army base, I couldn't help but feel a sense of vulnerability and uncertainty. My determination to uncover the reasons behind Vikrant's actions was unwavering, but I knew that the answers might bring even more complexity to our already tumultuous love story.

…

The phone call came at night, and as I heard Vikrant's voice on the other end of the line, a mixture of anticipation and anxiety welled up within me. I had been waiting for this moment, hoping to unravel the mystery behind his sudden change in behaviour. But what I heard was far from what I had expected.

'Pranali,' Vikrant's voice was firm and resolute, lacking the warmth and affection that had always defined our conversations.

His words sent a chill down my spine, and my heart seemed to skip a beat. I could sense the distance in his voice, a stark departure from the love and tenderness that had always defined our relationship.

He continued, 'I don't love you anymore, Pranali. It's best for both of us if we move on and never try to contact each other again.'

His words hit me like a tidal wave, and for a few moments, I was engulfed in a deep sense of despair. The man I had loved, the one who had promised to stand by my side, was now telling me to let go. I started sobbing as it was a pain unlike any other, a wound that seemed impossible to heal.

But even in that moment of heartbreak, a flicker of doubt crept into my mind. This wasn't the Vikrant I knew, the man who had shared my dreams and whispered promises of a future together. There had to be a reason behind this abrupt and cruel declaration.

Summoning all the strength I could muster, I replied, my voice trembling but determined, 'Vikrant, I don't believe this. The man I love would never say something like this without a reason. Please, tell me what's going on.'

I expected answers, but he disconnected the call. I couldn't accept this as the end of our love story, not without understanding the reasons behind his actions.

As I hung up the phone, sadness weighed heavily on my heart, but I also felt a newfound resolve. The Vikrant I knew wouldn't give up on our love without a fight, and I was determined to find out what had led to this abrupt and painful decision. Our journey was far from over, and I was prepared to face whatever challenges lay ahead in my quest for the truth and the restoration of our love.

…

By the way, that Dr. Sameer is none other than you.

❑

CHAPTER 12

The Truth Revealed

December 2016, Newtown Kolkata

As the months passed in silence, the absence of contact between Vikrant and me weighed heavily on my heart. I couldn't bear the thought of our love fading into oblivion, not without understanding the reasons behind his sudden decision to part ways. Tears in my eyes were all dried up. It was a painful and confusing time. I finally decided to bring this to an end.

'Vikrant,' I typed, 'My father is insistent that I consider marrying Dr. Sameer. After considerable thought, I have decided to go along with his wishes. I have no objections to marrying Dr. Sameer.'

As I sent the message, my heart ached at the prospect of feigning acceptance of a marriage that I had no intention of pursuing. But it was a necessary step, a ruse to re-establish contact with Vikrant and hopefully uncover the truth behind his actions.

I knew that this was a risky move, one that could further complicate our already complex situation. But I was determined to get to the bottom of the mystery.

As I anxiously awaited his response, I couldn't help but wonder how he would react to my message and whether it would lead us back to the path of reconciliation and understanding.

Vikrant's response came swiftly, and it was laced with a sense of finality that sent a shiver down my spine.

'I want to meet you for the last time.'

The words hung in the air, heavy with unspoken implications.

I knew that this meeting could be our last chance to unravel the mysteries that had driven us apart. It was a daunting prospect, but I couldn't let fear or uncertainty deter me. I had to see Vikrant, to look into his eyes and understand the reasons behind his drastic decisions.

With a sense of determination, I replied to his message, 'I agree to meet, Vikrant. Please, let me know when and where.'

...

'Vikrant, there's something I need to tell you. When I was in Mumbai, my father wanted me to consider marrying Dr. Sameer.' Vikrant's expression remained neutral, but a subtle shift in his eyes betrayed the depth of his emotions. He nodded.

Vikrant and I found ourselves in the serene surroundings resting ourselves on the same couch which is the evidence of our love in Victoria Garden. The beauty of the place was a stark contrast to the heaviness of our hearts.

As I continued to share the details of my father's wishes and the pressure I had felt during my visit to Mumbai, I noticed a glistening in Vikrant's eyes. His attempt to hide the tears that welled up was valiant, but I couldn't ignore the silent evidence of his pain.

I reached towards his hand.

'Vikrant,' I began, my voice filled with a mix of apprehension and determination, 'There are so many things I need to know. Why did you want to break up with me? Why did you stop loving me? Why haven't you contacted me all this time? Is there someone else in your life?'

Vikrant's eyes, once so warm and familiar, now held a hint of sadness as he replied, 'Pranali, it's not that simple. There are reasons, things I can't explain right now.'

I couldn't accept vague responses any longer. The uncertainty had tormented me for months, and I deserved clarity. 'Vikrant, please, I need to understand. And why did you want to meet me when I told you about Dr. Sameer? Why did tears well up in your eyes?'

'Vikrant look at me. Look into my eyes. Tell me the real truth. Am I not worthy to love ?'

'No, nothing like that.'

'Then why do you want to break up with me? Answer me. Vikrant...'

'Because your father told me to stay away from you, to keep my distance. He didn't want us to be together, to marry.'

His words hit me like a tidal wave, and my heart ached with the weight of his revelation. The man I loved had been forced to distance himself from me, not because he wanted to, but because of my father's wishes. It was a bitter truth to swallow, one that tore at the very core of our love story.

He looked away for a moment, as if collecting his thoughts. Then, with a heavy sigh, he said, 'Pranali, I didn't want to tell you this because I knew it would hurt you'

Tears welled up in my eyes as I struggled to comprehend the depth of Vikrant's sacrifice. He had chosen to bear the burden of my father's demand, all in the name of protecting me from pain.

Without hesitation, I threw my arms around Vikrant, hugging him tightly, and tears streamed down my face. He held me just as tightly, and in that moment, words were no longer necessary to convey the depth of our emotions.

I looked into Vikrant's eyes, my heart filled with a renewed sense of love and determination. 'Vikrant, we can't let my father's wishes tear us apart. We'll talk to him, convince him that our love is worth fighting for.'

With a passionate kiss, our lips met in a fiery affirmation of our love and the determination to overcome the obstacles that had stood in our path. The pain of separation, the pain of silence, all faded away as we embraced each other with a renewed sense of purpose.

Victoria Garden bore witness to our love's rekindling flame, as we pledged to face the challenges ahead as a united front. Our love story, once marred by secrets and misunderstandings, was now infused with a renewed sense of hope and the unwavering belief that together, we could overcome any obstacle that life placed in our path.

❑

CHAPTER 13

An Eternal Love Story

January 2017, Newtown Kolkata

I was at my happiest point in existence. I was with a man who cherished me above all others. For me, it was like a lovely fairy tale. Although we were unable to regularly meet, we used to talk on the phone every day and exchange recollections. But he used to make time for me every weekend. Leisure that was exclusively for me.

He loved to play with my hair and kiss my forehead when I would perch on his thighs and hug him. He enjoyed kissing my fingertips, biting my neck, and pinching my waist. I enjoyed biting him and rubbing my cheeks over his.

When we met, on a Sunday, he gave me a black silk sari. He urged me to wear it to Captain Manish's anniversary party. He had a friend and comrade in Captain Manish. Vikrant thus requested that I attend his party.

I had on a black silk sari. I didn't particularly enjoy wearing saris, but he gave it to me anyway. How then can I refuse it? I was unable to comprehend what I saw when I looked in the mirror. I appeared to be quite lovely. Vikrant's face flashed on my phone screen as I was just taking a look at myself in the mirror. I answered the phone.

'Its time, please, I'm waiting,' he beckoned. Outside, he was holding out for me. However, I wished to capture some images of mine. 'Please, could you step up,' I asked.

'Why? It's too late now. You know, we have to buy a present,' he retorted.

I pleaded, 'Please come, no, please.'

'Okay, baba. Hold on, I'll come,' he retorted.

He checked the buzzer. I let the door open. He appeared more attractive than ever. He matched my sari with a three-piece black jacket. He recently began to develop a beard after I told him he looked hot with one. He was looking as scorching as the sun, as I previously stated. Between them, his infant pink lips glistened. He smelled wonderful, as usual.

I believe he also used gel to fix his well-groomed hair which was not as smooth as I had assumed. Because of their brief length, they gave the impression of being silky. When I discovered that his hair is similar to that of Sri Lankan bowler Lasith Malinga, or more accurately, like sheep, he showed me some pictures of his early life. Whatever, it suits him. His blue irises had a Venus-like radiance.

When he saw me, his eyes grew wider than normal. Also opened was his lips. I understood the reason. 'What happened,' I enquired of him.

He regained awareness and said, 'Aaa...' He entered, shut the door, and gave me a bear embrace.

'What are you doing, Vikrant?' I questioned, a playful smile curving my lips. He released me.

'Love,' he answered with a mischievous glint in his eyes, making my heart flutter.

I chuckled softly, my laughter echoing in the peaceful garden. 'I didn't summon you here to make out.'

His lips curled into a boyish grin, and he quirked an eyebrow. 'So why did you summon me here?'

I hesitated for a moment, gathering my courage before I spoke, 'Please snap my photos.'

Vikrant's expression shifted, a hint of surprise in his eyes. 'Well, but...'

I interrupted him with a teasing tone, 'But what?'

A sly smile tugged at the corners of his lips, and he said, 'I want one smooch per picture.'

I feigned annoyance, but my eyes sparkled with delight. 'Vikrant...'

He continued with a playful grin, 'Offer... closes... soon.'

I had no choice but to say, 'All right, I'll do that.' He captured my 13 images and received my 13 kisses as payment. My lipstick caused his cheeks turn red. I instructed him to clean it. He reacted to my command by saying, 'Certainly, ma'am.'

We were moving forward. It was after 8pm I asked curiously, 'Hey Vikrant, tell me something about captain Manish.'

'Captain Manish is my closest friend,' he said. 'Together, we joined PARA SF and carried out numerous dangerous operations. The previous year, he wed Sagrika.'

'All right,'

'But do you know what?'

'What?' I questioned.

'He had a crush on a woman named Priyanka. He promised her that he would marry her when he finished the mission and returned. They used to discuss every detail of their days during daily video calls. They also made plans for the future.

'She abruptly ceased calling him though. The connection was lost entirely. He was unable to comprehend why she had experienced what she had. So, after finishing the task, he made the decision to meet her. But the task took too much time. He learned that Priyanka had wed someone else when he came back.'

'Ohh... so sad,' I exclaimed.

'Yes, at that point he was really shattered.' In an instant, all his aspirations faded away. He is content now, 'And I believe Sagrika is the right partner for him.'

In front of the gift store, Vikrant came to a stop. Our offering had to be accepted. Vikrant had a call as soon as we walked into the store, so he left and instructed me to choose a lovely gift. However, I was baffled. There were numerous present options. I therefore requested the shopkeeper to demonstrate a gift to give a married couple. He displayed a Radha Krishna Idol Showpiece with Diya for Puja and Household Decor in a Peacock Design. The exquisite handcrafted antique Lord Krishna Radha idol with gold plating on the sturdy metal stand was fashioned entirely of metal. Standing elegantly on the arch are Radha and Krishna. It was nicely finished and had a lovely pattern on the carving. The idol was golden polished, giving it a seductive ancient appearance. I really enjoyed it. Vikrant liked it too. So we bought it.

As soon as we got back on our way, I began daydreaming about the day that Vikrant and I would mark our first anniversary, followed by our tenth, twenty-fifth, and then our one hundredth. Although there was a lot of anticipation, those ideas were surprisingly comforting. I grinned as I turned to face Vikrant. He became aware of it.

'What happened?' he enquired.

'Nothing,' I answered.

He responded, 'Okay,'

'Vikrant, I love you.'

He added, 'I love you too, Prano.'

I innocently pleaded with her, ‘Please never leave me.’

‘Never’, he replied. We arrived at the gathering location, which was a hall. I held of Vikrant’s arm, and we went inside. We appeared to be a married pair. There were numerous additional Army commanders and their families in attendance.

I asked with hopeful eyes, ‘Does an army man have permission to reside with their family?’

‘It varies, though. We can have our families reside with us at Army headquarters if we are stationed in civil areas like this. However, if we are stationed in a border area, we do not have permission for it,’ he said.

‘You are late, Mr. Vikrant,’ someone said, pointing at us.

‘Ohh so sorry you know this ladies,’ Vikrant said. Both of them chuckled.

‘What do you mean by women?’, I asked. They were quiet for a moment and then laughed again.

‘Ok, meet him, he is Captain Manish.’ He was a tall, attractive man (not more than Vikrant).

‘Good to meet you,’ he greeted me. ‘Mrs. Shergil.’

I blushed.

Mrs. Shergil... Pranali Vikrant Shergil. Whoa.

Vikrant ruined my mood by saying, ‘No, we’re not married yet,’ and you know why.

I said, ‘I want to meet Sagrika Ma’am.’

‘Of course. But, she doesn’t appreciate hearing mam words from a woman her age, though,’ Manish added.

‘Okay,’ I said with a grin.

He named her ‘Sagrika.’ Looking at her face, I was genuinely shocked and perplexed. Her burnt half-face was visible. I was completely perplexed. Why was her face burnt? Why is the incident behind her face burnt? There were numerous inquiries, but only Vikrant had the knowledge to respond. I chose to ask him this question on the way home because it wasn't the appropriate time to do so.

We gave Manish and Sagrika their gift after they had cut the cake. The party started. As everyone else was dancing, my boyfriend was having a romantic moment. He kept putting his hands on my waist. I have no idea what transpired to with that evening. To dance, Manish and Sagrika invited us.

'May I have the honour of dancing with you, my lady?' Vikrant requested while kneeling down. Quietly, I stretched out my hand. He seized it and drew me in his direction. My body bumped up against his powerful one. My lips were trembling a little, and his gaze were following every inch of my body. He brought my body close to his and his hands firmly clasped my hands as the music changed to a very slow, calming tone. We were twirling. He drew my body further closer by putting his arms around my waist. On my face, I felt his warm breath.

...

The party finally ended, and we were heading back to our house. I decided now was the perfect opportunity to explain my confusion.

'What happened to Sagrika's face, Vikrant?' I questioned.

'Manish and Sagrika were classmates, and Manish was Sagrika's first love. But here's the twist: Manish had his heart set on Priyanka. Sagrika didn't know that at first, so she tried really hard to get close to Manish. She even wrote a love letter to confess her feelings, but Manish told her that he liked Priyanka.

'This made Sagrika pretty sad, but she still cared about Manish a lot. When Priyanka left him, Sagrika was the one who understood him the best. Manish realized that Sagrika was the only person who could love him so deeply. So, he eventually asked her to be with him, and she said yes. But life had other plans, and Manish had to go far away for some reason. However, true love doesn't care about distance. They managed to stay in touch, even though there were several network issues where Manish was. He tried his best to let Sagrika know he was fine.

'But then, something strange happened. Sagrika suddenly stopped calling him and didn't reply to his messages. Manish was worried and didn't understand why she was acting like this. We all realized that there was a big misunderstanding going on. I told Manish to find Sagrika and talk to her. That way, everything would become clear. Love can be tricky, but it's worth figuring out.

'Manish arrived at Sagrika's home after returning to his village. A person unlocked the door. She was Sagrika with half face burned. Manish was simultaneously delighted and surprised. Sagrika cried as she hurried into her bedroom. Sagrika's mother confronted him and related the incident to him. Her face was burned when a petrol tank accident occurred in her kitchen.

"So why is she not talking to me?" he questioned.

"Because she feels that you shouldn't be marrying a lady with burns on her face. She really cares about you. She was questioned about wanting to get married. You are the only individual she loves," she told him.

'It made all his ambiguity apparent. He grinned slightly before entering the bedroom. At the corner, Sagrika was weeping. Will you marry me? Manish asked her with his palm gently resting over her burned face. Sagrika collapsed and gave Manish a tight hug. "Sagrika, I love your hearts. And if you value someone's spirit, appearances are irrelevant. Sagrika, will you marry me?" Manish enquired.

"Sure," Sagrika affirmed while crying. And today is their first anniversary. They were married in a temple on the same day.'

'All right,' I retorted.

He left me at my house. This is the epitome of true affection, isn't it? Manish is accurate. When you love a person's soul, appearances don't count.

❑

CHAPTER 14

The Fact is, He is a Para Commando

April 2017, Newtown, Kolkata

'Hi, my sweet boyfriend. What are you doing?'

I blushed when he said, 'Missing my girlfriend.' He inquired, 'Can we meet tomorrow?'

'What?' I said amazed, 'I was going to ask you the same thing,' I added.

'Oh then Victoria Garden?'

'All right then, see you,' I replied. 'I love you,' I added.

'Love you so much,' he responded.

I replied, 'I know, my beloved friend.'

I wished to give my beloved boyfriend a gift. What then should I do? The query was that. I gave it a lot of consideration.

I looked everywhere. I then remembered Vikrant telling me once how much he adores timepieces. I'm done now! I chose to present him with a timepiece. I looked around, made a decision on an Audemars Piguet Royal Oak Perpetual Calendar watch, and placed my purchase. Even though it was very costly, who cares? I carried my Kohinoor Diamond. The purchase arrived to me after four days. I was overjoyed because it was the first time I had given him a present. I called him on the phone.

It was finally time. I chose to wear a black silk saree that my spouse had given me. I didn't clip my hair up because I had straightened it. I applied some cosmetics and was prepared to leave. I remembered to bring a present. To be frank, I was in a mood that evening. I wished to embrace him. I wanted to kiss him, strip him off, and then attack him. I had a special desire for his physique over mine. And I can almost guarantee that he shared my desire.

At 6 o'clock I arrived at Victoria Park. It was now dark. The wind was blowing cold, which enhanced my amorous mood. Vikrant, however, had not yet arrived. He is very careful with his time, so I found this to be quite a surprise. I looked through my handbag for my phone in order to see where he was. Fuck !! I had left it behind at home. I was left with no choice but to wait.

Vikrant had not been seen in 30 minutes. What's going on? Why didn't he come? Is he otherwise engaged? My thoughts raced with questions. But I was at a loss for words. I made the decision to delay some more. Even though it was 8 pm, Vikrant was still nowhere to be found. At the same moment, I was terrified, angry, and upset.

Why did he not turn up? I couldn't stop asking myself this one question. I was an utter idiot and left my phone at home. As a result, there was no means to reach him. Should I visit the Army's top brass? The plan didn't seem to be very effective. So I gave up on it. I decided to return home hurt. I was so upset that I couldn't stop weeping as I travelled. I arrived at my house. I put my bike in the garage and let myself in. My first action was to examine my mobile phone. Vikrant had left 33 missed calls for me. To view his texts, I opened WhatsApp.

"Baby, what's going on? Why haven't you been returning my calls? I'm truly sorry, but I have some devastating news to share. My commanding officer summoned me this afternoon and ordered me to report to Leh immediately. It was an urgent mission, and I had no choice but to comply. According to our intelligence, some Pakistani troops have crossed into our territory and are plotting something significant. They've even taken control of some of our bunkers, and this situation is unacceptable.

There are 45 Rashtriya Rifles troops stationed there, but the commanding officer believes that this mission should be entrusted to the Para Special Forces, with me as the mission's commander. I see this as an opportunity to prove my abilities and dedication. I'm truly sorry for not being able to meet you before I left. I know you won't easily forgive me for this, but please try to understand. I've said it before, and I'll say it again, for an Indian soldier, the country always comes first.

I've tried calling you multiple times, but you weren't answering, so I decided to write you this message. Being in a relationship with a soldier comes with its challenges. I might not always be by your side, but I will always hold you in the highest regard. I want to provide you with all the comforts in the world, but you also need to learn how to take care of yourself. It's crucial because only when you can look after yourself will this soldier be able to protect his motherland, his first love.

I can't say for certain when I'll be back, but I promise you I will return. You know something? For the first time, I'm feeling afraid, and it's because of you, not the mission. Prano, please be cautious and work hard. There might be some network issues preventing me from reaching you. Once again, I'm truly sorry. I have to go now. Prano, goodbye. Stay safe. Take care. Thank you. I love you deeply."

After reading this message, I felt completely broken inside. I was alone, without Vikrant and I had no idea when he would turn up. I thought I was in a fairy tale, but then reality struck me. He is, in reality, a Para Commando. When you recognise that you have met your soul mate and want to spend the remainder of your life with him. Then, you want to begin living the rest of your life as soon as possible because if that person were to abruptly pass away, your life's meaning would also. When you reach that low point in life, all you want is to be left alone.

My feet died, and I am now on the earth.

'Not again…..,' I shouted.

My eyes were crying, and I was crying. I was in tears. I was simultaneously irate, sad, and terrified. I sobbed before going to sleep. I stood up, sobbed once more, and then went back to sleep.

It continued non-stop for two days. I skipped lunch, dinner, and anything else. I didn't even leave that spot.

My door ranged, 'Tring... tring...' I was so exhausted that I couldn't move. I did, however, managed to unlock the entrance. 'Vikrant is he here?' I let the door open. Vikrant didn't attend. Shivam, Sonal, and Pratik instead stood there.

I said, 'Ohh.. you people.. come in.'

'Prana, what's wrong? View yourself.' Sonal immediately started making inquiries as soon as they entered in the room.

'What happened to you, Pranali?' Sonal said.

'Please be sited,' I said to her.

Shivam commanded 'Prana, tell us what happened.'

'Yes, you missed two days of work. Even worse, you didn't return our messages. Prana, what's wrong?' Pratik said, 'You can share with us.' Sonal was seated next to me.

'Guys, nothing,' I replied.

Sonal gently touched my forehead with her palms. 'Prana, look at you. Your pupils have enlarged. It is obvious that you hadn't slept for several evenings. Is anything regarding Vikrant happened? You can share with us.' After hearing her, I lost control of my emotions. As I hugged her, I started to sob.

'Ohh.. Shu... It's All right.' Sonal urged me not to weep. 'Pratik, please fetch a cup of water.'

'Who? Me?' asked Pratik. He was given a death look by Sonal. He said, 'Alright,' and then he brought me a cup of water.

'Ok, tell me now.' I told them the entire tale. How Vikrant left me and fled for the border. Before Sonal interrupted the silence between the three of them, there was some brief silence. 'Listen, Prana; in actuality, you are Vikrant's lover and he is a Para Commando. As a result, you must face the reality that you will encounter situations of this nature frequently. To safeguard the country, he must depart from you and cross international borders. Tell me one thing: Should he prioritise your well-being over carrying out his missions?'

I retorted, 'He should focus on his duties.'

'Right. However, how could he if you don't look after yourself?' I was at a loss for words. 'He'll be secure. I'm certain. It's now up to you to show that you merit the title of Army wife.' Shivam advised me to move on and embrace reality.

Pratik questioned, 'And tomorrow you're coming to work, right?'

'Yes, I'll be there.' I am truly fortunate to have them in my life. I had to face the fact that situations of this nature are typical of living as an army spouse. I must therefore get used to it. I made the decision to stop crying and to start living. The following day, I returned to work.

...

He hadn't been seen for thirty days. My existence was so flavourless. I had to stay living, so I did. I needed to be in top condition for Vikrant's comeback. I was looking to attempt something new to pass the time and divert my attention. I then began to watch anime. Actually, I didn't care much for anime, but

Vikrant did. I viewed anime films with the title 'a silent voice' as a test. It tells the tale of a former bully who became an outcast and chooses to get in touch with and become friends with the deaf girl he once teased.

I watched more anime movies, which subsequently piqued my interest. I wished to sample some anime shows. Naruto. Vikrant liked it a lot. He was enraged by it. Can you imagine a para commander tried to mimic the anime character all the time? However, it was real. When I discovered that it includes 720 episodes, my mouth remained open. twenty minutes each. It was a long journey. Yes, the series is very long, but it is well worth viewing. It describes affection, friendship, and aspirations.

I'll stop talking about anime now; let's get to my tale. My days consisted of getting up, going to work, coming home, watching cartoons, reading a book, and going to bed. not another.

I was working in my workplace late at night when an email notification appeared. When I checked it by opening it, imagine what? Vikrant sent the text in question. I rushed to open it.

Dear Pranali,

What's up? I'm aware that you're both happy and furious. You ought to be furious with me. Very apologetic. You love me, I'm sure of it. What's going on in your life? Is everything okay? I ask that you look after yourself.

On the Indian side of the LOC, the Pakistani Army dispatched troops to take a few positions. Four to seven companies of the Northern Light Infantry and members of the elite Special Services Group established bases on 132 strategic locations within the Indian-controlled area. Some reports claim that Afghan mercenaries and Kashmiri guerrillas support these Pakistani troops. The situation is dire, but I have faith that we will prevail.

I miss you a lot Prana. I particularly miss the Biryani you prepared. I just need this mission to be completed so I can enjoy your homemade biryani. I must leave now, so goodbye. Take care.

Yours,

Vikrant.

I clicked on compose option and started writing.

Dear Vikrant,

I miss you when I wake up. I miss you when I'm at work. I miss you before I go to sleep. Every minute of every day, I think about you and miss you. You are on my mind both when I wake up and when I go to bed. I'm currently deeply engaged. I can no longer imagine living without you.

When I got your note on that particular day. I was simultaneously very upset and furious. I asked, 'How can you treat me like this?' How can you go without even saying goodbye to me? In fact, those few days were very difficult for me. I had the impression that my spirit had been exiled from my body. But then, thanks to Sonal, Shivam and Pratik. They brought Pranali back, you know, and they helped me get out of my downbeat frame of mind. To have companions like them is truly a blessing.

I recently picked up a new pastime. anime viewing. Yes, I used to dislike anime, but now I can't exist without it. And just so you know, Mr. Vikrant, I finished Naruto in 41 days. Aren't I fantastic? I am extraordinary, yes. I had also read many books.

All right, enough already. We should discuss ourselves. You have my utmost admiration, Vikrant. My current boyfriend, who will one day become my spouse, is guarding his country's borders. Pizza is being joyfully consumed by those around me because my boyfriend is serving his motherland while famished.

I've discovered how much I love you over the past few days. What an Army Wife is supposed to be like. Vikrant, when are you coming back. I mean, please finish your assignment and come see me as soon as you can. You give me my breath. Without you, I can not live.

I want to tell you many things. But I don't believe this is the appropriate moment to tell you about it. You obviously lack biryani. However, I guarantee that I will prepare it and serve you with my own hands when you arrive. Ok. I believe that's sufficient.

Serve your country by concentrating on your tasks. I am not going anywhere. Complete your mission and return as soon as possible. Your jaan is waiting for you :(

Only yours,

Prana

...

Someone rang the doorbell at 11pm in the late hours. I was terrified. who is currently present. I took up the broom and began moving slowly in cat steps towards the entrance. When I opened the door, I was surprised to see Nimrit standing there.

I asked, 'Nimrit you?,' simultaneously pleased and surprised. I pleaded her to enter. She's here, why? Is everything okay?' Why didn't she inform me prior to arriving? I waited till she was at ease.

'What a treat, Nimrit. How are things going for you?'

She asked, appearing to be nervous, 'Fine. you?'

I responded, 'I'm fine, but why are you here and why didn't you tell me before coming?'

'Sorry about that. I recently misplaced my phone along with all the contacts on it. Therefore, I was unable to reach you.'

'All right,' I responded.

'How's your work going,' I enquired.

I was utterly shocked to hear 'I resigned.'

'Yet why? When you were promoted, you appeared to be truly perplexed How are you able to do this, Nimmi?'

'Yes, you are correct. When I was promoted, I was ecstatic. However, I was unaware at the time that this new chance would cost me my peace, my happiness, my privacy, and my personal space. I had to share a room with three men when I got to Bengaluru. I asked for a different room, but it was in futile. I never felt at ease around those people. I've always felt uneasy around their irises. But I managed to get some home. I considered the office to be excellent and highly evolved. However, internal politics and levels of favouritism were very high. My talent was never recognised by them. I was never given credit for my talent. For them, money was the only thing that mattered. The only thing that went well for me was that I kept in touch with Shivam. He was a huge assistance to me and was sensitive to my emotions.

'But when credit for a project for which I hadn't slept for a night was awarded to a man who didn't even know the project's specifics, my head began to fill with water.

'It's enough, I told myself. I penned a resignation letter and threw it on my manager's face before leaving Bengaluru.' I paid close attention.

I said with a nod, 'You know what, I believe I would have done the same if I was on your property.' She grinned too. 'So what's next?' I asked.

'Abhishek, my childhood friend and the science teacher, told me that their school needs a computer teacher,' she responded.

'Will you join it,' I asked.

She remarked, 'Yes, I am aware that the income will be lower, but I will be at peace.'

I said, grinning, 'Okay.'

'And I'm also going to speak to Shivam about our wedding,' she added.

'Are you serious?' I gushed.

'Hmm,' was her reply.

'That's a really wise choice,'

'Vikkie Bhaiyya is indeed on a quest. When he returns, I will tell him too'

He'll be overjoyed, I predicted. For a while, neither of us said anything. She continued to hold my palm. 'Do you miss him?'

I lied and smiled, 'No.'

She raised her right eyebrow as if to question me, 'Really?'

'I do miss him. I really do mourn him. When someone phones, the first thing I think is, 'Is Vikrant calling?' When the doorbell sounds, I wonder if Vikrant is home. But each time, my anticipation is dashed. I mourn him when I see Pratik and Sonal fighting. I ponder when the time will come when he and I also get into these ridiculous arguments. You know, the first few days after he left were really awful for me. I went two days without eating or drinking, but Sonal, Pratik, and Shivam helped me pull myself out of my melancholy,' I said, wiping a few tears from the corner of my eyes.

'Don't worry,' Nimrit assured me, 'He would be back shortly.'

'I'm aware of it.' We continued to converse before going to bed. I looked to see if Vikrant had sent me any emails. I avert my teary eyes after having my expectations dashed once more.

We had a small gathering the following day after Sonal, Pratik, Sid and Shivam arrived to meet Nimrit. Nimrit couldn't wait to meet Sid. Shivam felt uneasy because they had a strong connection there. When Nimrit noticed it, she called Shivam on the terrace where they had fun and cut off her conversation with Sid. She informed me that Shivam approved of their marriage after they spoke about it. Like me, they now simply anticipated Vikrant's return.

After a few more days, Nimrit had to move out of my house because it was time for her to go. I left her at the airport. She abandoned me once more after joining us along with Sonal Pratik and Shivam. Again, I was by myself. I had once more fallen. Nimrit spent three days with me. Those were lovely times. Those three days resembled an island of tranquilly surrounded by a sea of sorrow. I was once more lost in the ocean of sorrow and solitude. I had a suffocating sensation. I unlocked the door because I needed to leave. Sid, however, was present to my astonishment.

I said, keeping my palm on my heart, 'Ohh Sid, you scared me.'

'Am I looking terrible?' I chuckled. 'No, no, I didn't mean to say that.'

'May I come in?'

'Ohh.. sorry.. please come in.'

'I just happened to be passing by so I thought we should meet.'

'Thank you for coming.' I said in a hushed voice, 'I really needed someone.'

'Are you all right?'

'Yes I am'.

'Really?'

'Should I tell him about Vikrant?'

'Yes, nothing,' I replied.

'Okay,' he grinned. When he departed, we had a satisfying conversation. Again, I was by myself. There seems to be a gap, in my opinion. It is what? Vikrant. Yes. Why did I join this company? Why did I meet Nimrit? Why did I meet Vikrant? Why did I give him my cell phone number? Why did I adore him and still do? I experienced suffocation once more.

❑

CHAPTER 15

Something Worth Waiting For

July 2017, Newtown, Kolkata

It was 7pm. when someone ranged my door. 'Is Sid back? Has he forgotten something,' I wondered. The only way I could learn the solutions was to open the door. When I opened the door to look around, a tall man stood there holding a sizeable arrangement of roses. Instead, he purposefully concealed it. He was carrying one suitcase as well.

'Who is he?' My inner voice said, 'He is definitely not Sid.'

'Who are you?' I questioned.

He responded, slowly stepping back from the bouquet to show his face, 'Your boyfriend.' I couldn't comprehend what I was seeing. He was actually my spouse. You got it correctly—Vikrant was standing there holding a sizable bouquet—possibly numbering 100 roses. I had broad open eyes. I took a few strides backwards.

'Is he actually present? Or is this just in my head?' I thought to myself.

He entered and shut the door after him. I still couldn't believe he was standing so close to me and asked, 'Vikrant, are you really here?'

He replied, 'Yes Prana, I am here.' I started sobbing in relief. He dropped a bouquet and his luggage as I squeezed him tightly. I began giving him a really ardent kiss. My perceptions all left me. He held of my neck with his right hand and my back with his left. He drew me even nearer to him. His tongue was battling with mine in my mouth. That one kiss was the culmination of the suffering buried deep within our hearts. Even though we were both silent, our lips were speaking.

'Please don't abandon me once more.' My lips encountered his and said, 'I can't live without you.'

'Yes, Prana, I won't ever abandon you.' His lips said to mine, 'I am only yours and you are only mine.' We kissed for at least fifteen minutes. It took me just long enough to become aware. I let go of him and took two steps away. He moved closer to me while carrying a bouquet and a suitcase.

He handed it to me and said, 'This is for you, my jaan.'

I said, 'Thank you, Vikrant, for coming here,' allowing a few tears to leave my eyes. I requested him to rest on sofa. I sat next to him and kept a bouquet on a neighbouring table. I gently seized his visage.

'What's up, Vikrant?' I noticed some alterations in his features. His beard and hair were both very lengthy. His cheeks were more red now . His blue irises still had the same glow, though.

'I am just fine. Tell me, how are you?' he asked.

'I'm fine, too.' He put his right palm on my thigh and relaxed.

'Sorry for everything, Prana.'

‘For what?’ I questioned.

‘I walked away from you. When you needed me, I wasn’t there. The suffering you’ve endured as a result of me.’ He felt bad and said, ‘So sorry for it.’

‘Vikrant, you shouldn’t feel bad. I am not a regular man’s partner. I am a Para Commando’s partner. This means that I will encounter these circumstances frequently in my life and that I must grin while handling them.’

‘Thank you, Prana,’ he said with a grin and I nodded.

‘So how did the operation go?’ I asked after a few brief seconds of silence.

‘The mission was fantastic, but a terrible thing occurred after the mission,’ he said.

‘What are you saying?’ I questioned.

‘As the sun dipped below the horizon, casting shadows over the rugged terrain of Leh and Ladakh, my team and I were poised for a mission laden with complexity and danger. We had received intel that Pakistani troops had infiltrated military bunkers in the region, but the situation was further compounded by the involvement of the Lashkar-e-Ghazi terrorist organization. It was approximately 7pm. when we commenced our search operation, unaware of the challenges that awaited us.

‘The weather added an element of unpredictability to our mission, with thick fog enveloping the landscape and severely limiting our visibility. This atmospheric obscurity would soon prove to be both a bane and a boon.

‘The terrain guided us to a cluster of houses where we discovered what seemed to be discarded items concealed between the boundary walls of neighbouring homes. Suspicion hung in the air, and our mission had taken an ominous turn.

‘One of my fellow soldiers pointed out, ‘Sir, look, there are some footprints here.’ It was the critical juncture we decided to follow those tracks, unknowingly leading us into the heart of our adversaries.

‘However, the enemy lay in ambush, fully aware of our movements. Suddenly, their gunfire erupted from inside the homes, and we found ourselves caught in the open with no immediate cover. The situation grew increasingly perilous, and it was evident that our foes had planned and executed this assault with precision.

‘In response, I ordered my soldiers to seek refuge behind nearby trees while we exchanged gunfire with the enemy. Our covering fire provided some protection, but the battle was far from over.

‘The terrorists had honed in on three specific houses, and my team was poised for a decisive move. We breached the rear doors of these homes, plunging into the unknown, where darkness and danger coexisted. The tactical and strategic training of my team came to the forefront as we navigated these treacherous interiors.

‘Amidst the chaos and the intensity of the battle, I spotted a terrorist attempting to flee. My training and instincts guided me, and I took my shot, incapacitating the adversary. It was a chilling moment, but there was no time for contemplation as the battle raged on.

‘Realizing that they were losing ground, the terrorists launched a final, desperate assault. They detonated explosives within all three houses, leading to the tragic loss of nine of my comrades. I raced to the scene in hopes of finding survivors, but the aftermath was a scene of devastation, and the fallen soldiers left an indelible mark on my soul.

‘Within the dimly lit aftermath, I heard a faint voice, which drew me to a severely wounded terrorist, the very one I had incapacitated earlier. I kept my weapon trained on him as I sought information from our adversary, unravelling the extent of the tangled web we had entered. His admission confirmed our suspicions: "Lashkar-e-Ghazi."

“Who controls it?”

“Maqsood,” was his response.

‘I yelled “Maqsood” again and shot him. Ram Gopal, our signalman, notified our headquarters of the circumstance.

Retaliation-fuelled flames tore through me. At this point, my only goal is to murder Maqsood and eliminate Lashkar-e-Ghazi. I don't know who this murderous Maqsood is, but he needs to get ready because Captain Vikrant the tiger is coming for him.

'As dawn broke on the following day, we stood resolute and prepared for the challenging task ahead. We were divided into 20 teams, each assigned to reclaim the vital bunkers. I assumed command of Bravo Company, well aware of the arduous nature of our mission. The militants held the high ground advantage, positioned atop the hill, and the odds were stacked against us. To maintain the element of surprise, we made the strategic decision not to use helicopters, instead choosing to cover the 77-kilometre journey on foot.

'With determination etched on our faces, we embarked on our gruelling journey towards the enemy's shelters. We reached our destination, and through the lens of my binoculars, I could observe their positions. Yet, the timing was not yet right; we needed the shroud of nightfall to cloak our actions. My soldiers stood prepared, their resolve unwavering.

'Despite the biting cold wind that turned the weather unfavourable, our unwavering spirit kept us moving forward. As dawn neared, we found ourselves within striking distance of the enemy, who remained blissfully unaware of our presence. The moment had arrived, and I gave the order to encircle and capture them. But the silence was soon shattered by enemy gunfire. We sought refuge behind the protective embrace of large boulders, forced into a defensive position against their tactical advantage and numerical superiority.

'With no other recourse, I commanded a frontal assault, and my team provided covering fire as I led the charge from the rear. Two of my brave soldiers stood at my side as we executed our strategy, infiltrating the bunkers where six enemy combatants were entrenched. We were only three, but our determination and courage carried us forward. Hand-to-hand combat unfolded in the close quarters of the bunkers, and through unwavering resolve, we emerged victorious.

'After retaking the bunkers and eliminating the enemy threat, we triumphantly raised the Indian flag atop the slope. Our signalman, Ram Gopal, swiftly communicated our success to headquarters, marking a momentous achievement.

'The following day, fortified by a night of rest, we forged onward, marching to reclaim the second bunker and then the third. The other companies, Charlie and Alpha, also accomplished their respective objectives. With determination, unwavering courage, and a united spirit, India emerged victorious in the battle. The tri-colour flag fluttered in the wind, a symbol of our success and unwavering commitment to our homeland.'

'That's great,' I said, quietly and attentively taking in the entire narrative. I kissed him and told him, 'Vikrant, I'm so proud of you. Oh, apologies, I meant "Captain Vikrant",' I said.

I was shocked when he said, 'Actually the thing is I am not a Captain in the Indian Army anymore.' I let him go.

'What are you saying, Vikrant?'

'I'm no longer Captain Vikrant,' he said again.

'But why?'

'Because now... I'm Major Vikrant Shergil,' he replied.

He announced proudly, 'I got a promotion Prana, and now I'm Major Vikrant Shergil.'

'Vikrant, congratulations! I'm so happy for you.'

'Thank you.'

'But I'm perplexed. Why did you claim that a horrible incident occurred following the mission?' He remained silent for a short while longer before continuing the narrative.

'We began our journey back to Headquarters, the three victorious companies marching together. We formed a 49-man military unit, a formidable force bolstered by our recent achievements. As the sun descended on the horizon, we decided to establish our camp for the night. Our chosen location was near a waterway, and we decided to set up two camps to accommodate the troops. One camp, consisting of 25 soldiers, was positioned on the hill, while the other camp, housing 24 troops, was established by the riverbank.

'Despite the prevailing calm, a sense of unease still hung in the air. I took a moment to rest in the hillside shelter, contemplating the remarkable events that had transpired. In the stillness of the night, our peaceful respite was suddenly disrupted.

'Shortly after midnight, our world was jolted by an unexpected earthquake, and its seismic waves shook us from our slumber. When I attempted to peer outside, I was met with a disorienting sight—the surroundings were enveloped in a thick shroud of falling snow, and fierce winds howled through the night. Darkness held sway, and our world became an abyss of uncertainty.

'In the morning light, the astonishing revelation awaited us. Our second campsite had disappeared entirely. A mystical surge in water levels had wrought havoc on our camp, sweeping away not only the tents and supplies but also the 24 soldiers who had been stationed there. It was a scene of utter devastation. It was then that I discovered a deformed body, roughly 50 kilometres from our campsite.

'The most unsettling aspect of this discovery was the impossibility of identifying the body. It lay scattered in pieces, with internal organs strewn across the terrain. In the absence of visual cues, we were compelled to resort to blood tests for the purpose of identification.

'Pranali, can you imagine the profound sadness that overcame us? The previous night, those very troops had celebrated their hard-fought victory, rejoicing with song and dance. Yet, their jubilation had been ephemeral, crushed by the capricious hand of fate.

'One haunting truth continues to torment me—the fact that Maqsood remains alive because I was unable to exact retribution.

I firmly believe that the war will only conclude when I carry out the task of eliminating Maqsood and dismantling the purported terrorist group, Lashkar-e-Ghazi.'

I did not respond.

After a short while, I said, 'Hey Vikrant, do you know that Nimmi resigned from her job?'

'She sent me a note. She is a mature woman, but I was angry at her at first. She is wise enough to know what is best for herself, and I appreciate that.'

'Okay.'

My inner voice said, 'Nimmi is such a lucky girl to have a brother like him.'

'I still have some news for you.' Actually, I'm on vacation for 30 days. I have to return to Kashmir and report myself after that. because Kashmir is where I am currently posted.'

'What? So, will you abandon me again?' I innocently asked.

'Sorry. But I'll be secure. I won't be close to any boundaries. We'll stay in touch constantly. I'll phone you every day.' I was upset because I believed that he would never abandon me again, but I was mistaken. Everything will be fine until and unless Pakistani militants cross their limit.

He asked, 'You know something?'

'What?'

'When I get back next time, we're getting married.'

'Are you serious?' I asked overjoyed as my eyes lit up.

'Yes'

'Promise?' I was joyful once more when he said, 'I promise you that just after a few days and I will be completely yours. You know what, I'll set up and arrange Nimrit and Shivam's wedding before my vacation is over,' he continued.

'What?'

'Yes. I'll talk to Shivam and then his family tomorrow. If everything goes well, I'll set up their wedding.'

'That's fantastic,' I responded.

'Hey, look at what I got for you,' he said giving me his bag.

'What?' I took the bag he gave me and I opened it.

'What's this?' He purchased the poultry, rice, and basic biryani masalas.

I responded, 'Understood.' He pleaded and I nodded.

He followed me to the kitchen and said, 'I'll also assist you. He didn't assist me at all, to be honest. He constantly bothered me. But everything about him—his voice, his presence—made me happy. I proclaimed as I entered the dining room, 'Your biryani will be ready in 30 minutes.' We talked for a short while.

The biryani was prepared after 30 minutes. Its fragrance permeated the entire room. Vikrant's lips began to produce a lot of saliva, indicating how much he was craving the food. I said as I handed him the food, 'And your biryani is ready.'

When I intervened, he was just about to take the first mouthful. 'You are aware that I pledged to feed you with my hands. So please enable me to fulfil my promise now,' I said. 'Sure,' he smiled in response. I began feeding him food. His face indicated that Biryani had been amazing cooked. He was content. He was happy. So, I was happy.

At that time, he ate like a tiny infant. A young child was visible inside a ruthless para commando. A few tears broke free from my eyelashes and rolled onto my chicks. Vikrant caught it. "What happened," he questioned as his eyebrows shot up? I said, 'Nothing,' while shaking my head. He gave me an assent and began to feed me. I'll never forget that lovely time. I thought, "This is what I've been missing for the last few months."

We made the decision to go to the terrace after supper. It was a cloudless night. Numerous stars were visible to us. We both simultaneously referred to it as a 'shooting star' while looking at it. 'The stars are lovely, aren't they?' I said

He put his palm against my cheek and replied, 'Yes, but not more than you.'

'Ohh, really?' I laughed.

'Yes.'

The melody 'Tumse milke, aisa laga tumse milke, Armaan hue poori dil ke, Aai meri jaan-e-wafa' was playing when I took my phone out of my pocket. We began dancing the famous Salsa style, which is typically seen at events or dance clubs. We were totally engrossed in one another. We embarrassed each other when the performance was over. We stood there in silence, sensing the warmth and air of one another.

'I think I should leave now,' Vikrant said.

I tightened my embrace and said, 'No, please stay with me.'

'Prano....'

'Please...'

'All right, I'll stay here.'

'Thank you,' I said.

He gently scooped me up in his strong arms, carrying me over to the bedroom, where he gently lowered me onto the bed. As the night settled in around us, the ambiance was serene and intimate. We decided to indulge in the simple pleasure of watching a romantic Bollywood film together, and that in itself was enough to kindle a sense of shared affection and desire.

The movie played on, but as the storyline unfolded on the screen, another narrative began to take shape in the room. The romantic and tender moments between the characters on the television served as a catalyst for the emotions building between us. Our gazes locked, and an unspoken connection deepened with every passing moment.

The magic of that night didn't lie solely in the cinematic love story; it was the love story unfolding right there, in our hearts and in our shared glances. As the film reached its climax, our own story was about to begin.

To respect the intimacy of the moment, I'll spare you the more explicit details, but suffice it to say that our love expressed itself fully that night. It was a night of passion, tenderness, and a connection that transcended the physical. It was the kind of night you remember for a lifetime, one that imprints itself upon your heart and soul, etching every detail into your memory.

Afterwards, as the world outside fell into a peaceful slumber, Vikrant held me in his loving embrace. The feeling of being enveloped in his arms, with the rhythm of his heartbeat synchronizing with my own, was nothing short of pure serenity. It was there, in the safety of his embrace, that I felt as if I had found my sanctuary in the entire universe.

...

As the sun's gentle rays peeked through the curtains, I stirred awake, finding Vikrant still in a peaceful slumber beside me. He looked utterly charming and serene in his sleep, and I couldn't help but watch him, not wanting to disturb his rest.

With a careful, noiseless step, I left the bed and prepared myself for the day, taking a refreshing shower to start the morning. When I returned to the bedroom, Vikrant had awakened, and his eyes followed my every move as I entered the room. I couldn't help but smile at the adoration in his gaze.

In a playful gesture, Vikrant reached out and gently caught my hand, pulling me down to the bed beside him. I inquired with a hint of mischief, 'What are you doing?'

He simply responded with a charming smile, 'Romance.'

I laughed at his unexpected response and playfully protested, 'Leave me,' and he released his hold on my hand, allowing me to sit up.

As the morning progressed, Vikrant and I had the delightful opportunity to meet Shivam, who had chosen to marry Nimrit. The prospect of their union was heart-warming, and their love story had swiftly progressed. We engaged in a conversation with Shivam, discussing the impending marriage.

To our delight, he was more than willing to embrace the journey of matrimony, and his enthusiasm was mirrored by the approval of both our families. The green light from their loved ones made the process surprisingly swift, and their marriage was officially and joyously celebrated in a relatively short span of time. Love had triumphed, and a new chapter had begun for Nimrit and Shivam.

#Shivam_weds_Nimrit

❑

CHAPTER 16

Whispers of Longing

September 2017, Newtown, Kolkata

It was time after the marriage of Shivam and Nimrit. Vikrant moved back to Kashmir. The distance between us had stretched like an invisible thread, connecting two worlds that seemed impossibly far apart. While I stayed in the busy city of Kolkata, wishing for Vikrant's presence with each passing day, he was stationed in the rough terrain of Kashmir, performing his duties as a soldier.

Our phone discussions, where the sound of his voice carried echoes of the love we shared, gave me comfort as the days stretched into weeks. But the pain of being apart kept gnawing at my heart, serving as a continual reminder of the distance separating us.

I sat at the window one evening, taking in the familiar views of Kolkata as the sun started to set and shed a warm golden glow over the city. Fragments of conversations, children playing in the streets laughing, and distant traffic sounds were all carried by the soft air.

My fingers longed to call Vikrant's number so I could hear his voice and briefly overcome our great distance as I thoughtlessly traced the contours of my phone. But a voice inside pleaded with me to be patient, reassuring me of the significance of his obligations and the sacrifices he made on our behalf.

My phone buzzed, waking me out of my daydream as the evening started to wane into the embrace of dusk. As soon as I saw Vikrant's name flashing on the screen, my heart skipped a beat as excitement and eagerness surged through my body.

'Hello?' I responded with a voice that was tinged with both joy and longing.

Vikrant's voice resounded across the line, calling out 'Pranali' with a tone that mixed affection and exhaustion. 'I wish I was there to hold you tight and watch the sunset with you right now'.

Despite the pain in my heart, a smile tugged at the corners of my lips. 'You are missed, Vikrant. I feel incomplete without you at my side every day.'

When there was a little lull on the other end of the queue, I could feel his longing and see a reflection of it in mine. 'I know, Prana. Trust me, I share your sentiments. But we must persevere, for ourselves, for one another, and for our dreams.' His remarks struck a chord inside of me, reminding me of our shared ideals and the goals we had set for ourselves.

Our love deepened during those times when we were apart due to distance, fuelled by the difficulties we encountered and the power we found in one another. I could almost feel Vikrant's presence beside me as we spoke, as we shared the specifics of our days and the dreams that glistened in our hearts, as well as his consoling touch and unfailing support. Our chats connected our souls and provided a haven in the midst of separation by transcending the limitations of physical separation.

As the night grew darker, stars started to shine in the soft sky. We discussed our dreams and goals as well as the journeys we planned to take once we were back together. Weaving a tapestry of love and tenacity, the cadence of our talk danced to a song that only our hearts could hear. I found comfort in that chapter of yearning and hushed promises.

Our love overcame the limitations of time and space because it was strong and uncompromising. I knew our love was stronger than any barrier that attempted to keep us apart in those moments when the world outside of us seemed insignificant.

The room's emptiness became less oppressive when I said goodnight to Vikrant. Our relationship, fostered by our steadfast support and innumerable chats, gave me reason to hope. The path ahead might be difficult, but armed with love and resolve, we would confront the obstacles together, unwavering in our goal of a future in which our souls would once more entwine.

Days became weeks, and weeks became months, yet our relationship remained solid. Each chat turned into a lifeline, a priceless thread that united us despite the great distance separating us. We communicated over the distance by sharing experiences, tears, and laughter. But as time passed, the longing grew stronger.

I yearned to look at Vikrant, to feel his presence next to me, and to tightly hug him. The separation weighed heavily on my heart, an ever-present reminder of the sacrifices we both made for the greater good.

...

Sid's unexpected request left me curious and slightly apprehensive. When he inquired about my availability for the upcoming Sunday, I turned my attention toward him and responded with a simple, 'Yes.'

However, his next question, 'Can we visit Victoria Garden?' intrigued me further. Sid's request seemed out of the ordinary, and I couldn't help but wonder what he wanted to share, prompting me to inquire, 'Of course.'

His reply only deepened my curiosity. He revealed, 'I wish to share something with you, but this is not the appropriate forum.' This cryptic statement left me pondering the nature of the matter he wanted to discuss, and I couldn't help but feel a sense of mystery surrounding his request.

In response, I agreed to meet him at Victoria Garden on Sunday, acknowledging the need for a more suitable setting for the conversation he had in mind. As I confirmed our meeting, my inner voice echoed my thoughts, questioning the enigmatic revelation Sid was planning to make. The anticipation of what he wanted to share began to build within me, and I found myself counting the days till our meeting, eager to unravel the mystery he held.

...

At 5pm. on Sunday, Sid came to pick me and we headed to Victoria Garden. In the garden, I could sense the emptiness. Why was that the case? Yes, as it was the second occasion I had travelled here alone. The first was the time we chose to meet. However, he left to queue towards Kashmir without even informing me. This is the location of my first encounter with Vikrant. I proposed Vikrant here. And right here is where I gave him my first kiss. This location serves as a symbol of our affection. But at this point, Vikrant was not present.

As we arrived at Victoria Garden, I felt a mix of anticipation and curiosity, eager to uncover the mystery Sid had alluded to. I turned to him and urged, 'So tell me now.'

However, Sid's response left me puzzled. He seemed hesitant, struggling to find the right words. I pressed him, my patience waning, 'Sid, could you please be clear?'

Finally, he mustered the courage to convey his message, and his words left me stunned. He confessed, 'Actually, Pranali, I'm not sure where to start.'

Intrigued and perplexed, I implored him to continue, 'Okay, Sid, please be clear.'

And then came the revelation that I hadn't anticipated. Sid revealed, 'I've known you since you joined this business. I looked at your biography, and guess what? Now I love you.'

His confession left me in disbelief, and I could only manage to utter a bewildered, 'What?'

'I love you, Pranali. I love you so much. I desired to be near you. I desired to cooperate with you. I therefore requested dad that Nimrit be promoted and transferred to Bengaluru so that I may fill the vacancy. After Priya, you are the only girl I adored, Pranali. And I believe that we were meant to be together. We share the same interests and passions. Our interests are similar. This is an indication that our relationship is meant to be, and...'

'I have a boyfriend,' I began to feel awkward around his words, so I said it. He was in total shock and asked, 'What?' I informed him of my connection to Vikrant. He believed that Vikrant and I are merely friends. 'I cherish Vikrant. I adore him so much, and our relationship is very serious. Sid, you are a decent individual. I like you a lot. However, that does not imply that we can be a couple for life. Even though we share the same interests and passions, I am meant to be Vikrant's wife and your... just friend.' He remained silent for a short while.

'So you're rejecting me because you love that soldier who isn't with you.'

I asked. 'What do you mean?'

'He's going to be on missions all the time. How can he grant you his time?'

I said in a stern voice, 'You are going too far.'

'Pranali, this is the reality. He might be an excellent soldier, but he will never make a decent boyfriend. Because he himself doesn't know whether he will survive in his mission or....' I slapped him, which got everyone in the garden's notice.

'Enough, if you mention Vikrant once more, I'll murder you. Don't compare yourself with Vikrant. You'll never perform on his level. Vikrant can adore me more than anyone else on the planet, including you. Believe that.'

I went home after leaving the yard. I erred in my judgement. I ought to have informed him earlier about Vikrant. He was sorely missed by me. I was anxious to see Vikrant. I wished to talk to him. I wished to embrace him. How then could I? 'Shall I travel to Jammu? Yes, I ought to visit Jammu and inform him of Sid. I told myself, 'I should tell him that I want to marry him as soon as possible.'

...

The following day at work, I couldn't find Sid, but his confession of love was still fresh in my mind. However, I made no immediate effort to reach out to him or understand the situation. Instead, I decided to take some time off to sort through my thoughts and feelings.

I headed to Mr. Khanna's office and submitted a request for six days leave. It was a significant step for me since I had never asked for time off in all my years at the company. Mr. Khanna granted my request without much questioning, sensing that something important must be happening.

I also felt the need to confide in Sonal. I informed her about the unexpected revelation from Sid and the emotions it had stirred within me. Sonal, understanding and perceptive as always, admitted that she had sensed something like this might occur. She assured me that it was essential for me to sort out my feelings and take some time for myself.

With my leave approved and Sonal's understanding, I began planning my trip to meet Vikrant in Jammu. The first step was booking my flight from Kolkata to Jammu, which I managed to do swiftly. I deliberately kept this trip a surprise from Vikrant, wanting to see the joy and surprise in his eyes when I arrived. This trip was my way of finding some clarity about my feelings and a chance to reunite with the one person who had always held a special place in my heart.

❑

CHAPTER 17

The Beckoning of Kashmir

November 2017, Airport, Kolkata

I was seated in the reclining chair at Kolkata Airport at 2am Why? Because I had a flight to Jammu at 4.35 am. Even though it wasn't a vacation, my excitement was at its highest. Because I was finally going to meet Major Vikrant Shergil, my Para commando boyfriend, after five hard months.

A female next to me yelled 'Soham' when she saw a man coming her way.

That man shouted back, 'Meenal,' with equal intensity.

'Perhaps they are a couple,' I guessed.

They might have recently reconnected. She arrived to fetch him at 2am. with a large bouquet in her hand. They gave each other hugs. Their eagerness to meet was evident in their excitement, which ultimately made me remember the day I first met Vikrant.

I boarded the aircraft and found a spot. The flight was about to depart. My enthusiasm grew as the minutes ticked by. My anticipation for meeting Vikrant was growing. A lady sitting next to me questioned, 'Is this your first time on a plane?'

'No, I had only gone a few times,' I retorted.

'Oh, I see. You appear incredibly delighted. Do you intend to meet your partner in Jammu?'

'What?' I questioned a little eagerly, 'How did you recognise it?' She chuckled. 'Simply assumed.'

'Oh fine'.

'Actually, I'm heading to Jammu to meet my boyfriend.' When asked if he was a soldier too, she replied, 'No, he's an instructor.'

'All right'

'I'm Jasmine.'

'Pranali here. Nice to meet you.' We became friends instantly. Friends, having genuine friends is one of life's most priceless possessions. Our journey is only meaningful if we have friends, and having real friends can mean the world. They are the ones who back us when we need it, stick by us no matter what, and rejoice with us when we succeed. Hopefully, Nimrit, Sonal, Shivam, and Pratik will turn out to be some of my closest friends.

Jasmine questioned me, 'So how did you meet for the first time?'

'He is actually my friend Nimrit's older brother.'

'Wow, sounds interesting.'

'Same question for you.'

'Actually WhatsApp played a major role in the formation of our relationship,' were the responses I received.

'How?' I excitedly questioned.

'He is a schoolmate of mine. Since then, he has had feelings for me. But he never told me about it. After a year, he sent me a WhatsApp message, and our love tale officially began. Our friendship is currently distance-based. Therefore, our only communication is through WhatsApp. Thank you WhatsApp, hashtag.' She got absorbed in perusing the article. WhatsApp was also crucial in the beginning of my love

Jasmine enquired, 'Can I have your phone number?'

'Of course'. We swapped phone numbers.

She grinned and said, 'I'd like to hear your love story someday. Now that your eyes are looking red, I believe you should get some rest.'

'I appreciate your thoughtfulness and care.' I closed my eyes, but I couldn't help but think of Vikrant.

...

JAMMU,

Jasmine woke me up by saying, 'Pranali, wake up—we are now in Jammu.'

At 10:35am after a six-hour flight, I eventually arrived in Jammu. The city of Jammu is renowned for its breath-taking natural beauty, extensive cultural legacy, and spiritual importance. The city is encircled by snow-capped mountains, undulating hills, and lush woods as it lies in the foothills of the Himalayas.

The city's picturesque scenery is further enhanced by the Tawi River's winding path through it. Several ancient temples, including the well-known Vaishno Devi Temple, which draws millions of visitors each year, are also located in Jammu.

The vibrant, busy local bazaars provide a glimpse into the city's extensive cultural history. Discovering Jammu's historic sites, taking in its bustling street life, or simply taking in its breath-taking natural beauty will leave visitors in awe and surprise.

Jasmine gave me a bear hug and said, 'I'd like to meet you again.' She stepped inside the waiting taxi. I made the decision to eat breakfast at the neighbouring hotel so that I would be alert.

'What makes this place unique?' I questioned a server.

'Rogan Josh Mam'

'I had never heard of it before, what is it made of?'

'A well-known meat dish from Kashmir is Rogan Josh. A special combination of Kashmiri seasonings is used to flavour the spicy tomato and yoghurt sauce in which the tender meat is slowly cooked.'

'Okay, I'd like to give it a shot.' I bought it. I eventually heard the mayhem behind me. I looked in that direction to see that a select group of friends were commemorating a birthday.

...

Navigating the unfamiliar streets of Jammu in search of the Army Headquarters proved to be a daunting challenge. The city's layout and the military base's concealed location added to the complexity. Streets bustled with activity, and the bustling traffic did little to ease the situation. But with determination, I persevered, asking for directions and relying on landmarks.

The anticipation of reaching my destination and reuniting with Vikrant fuelled my resolve. Finally, after a series of twists and turns, I managed to locate the Army HQ, a triumphant moment in my quest to find him.

As I walked, I could see the Army Headquarters looming ahead, just 3 kilometres away. To cover the remaining distance more quickly, I decided to hop into a rickshaw. The ride took about 10 minutes, and as we approached the Para SF Army Headquarters in Jammu, it became evident why this location was known for its heightened security.

The headquarters was a fortress of secrecy and protection, designed to safeguard highly sensitive military operations and personnel. The exterior of the building was unassuming and practical, with a straightforward layout that emphasized functionality and security. Thick concrete walls enclosed the area, and high walls, along with a perimeter fence, created a formidable barrier to keep out unauthorized individuals. Throughout the premises, armed soldiers were stationed, maintaining a watchful presence.

As I approached the entrance, I couldn't help but feel a sense of trepidation. The formidable structure and the intense security measures were intimidating. I wondered how I would go about finding Vikrant in such a place, amidst all these security measures.

My uncertainty was compounded when I reached a large barrier at the entrance. I stood there, feeling somewhat lost and unsure of my next steps. The army officer stationed there noticed my hesitation and decided to halt me from entering further. My journey to reunite with Vikrant was met with its first challenge: gaining access to this highly secure military establishment.

The army officer sternly told me, 'Sorry, ma'am, but you can't enter inside.' I felt a bit disheartened by this roadblock.

But then, he seemed to recognize me and inquired, 'Actually, I'm here to meet Major Vikrant.'

'Wait, are you Pranali Sharma?'

'Yes.' It puzzled me how he knew my name, as I hadn't introduced myself.

With a warm smile, he revealed, 'I'm Manoj Patel, and Major Vikrant is a close friend of mine. He mentioned you.'

I couldn't help but wonder what Vikrant had told Manoj about me.

Still slightly bewildered, I stammered, 'Aamm... Where is he now?'

Manoj informed me, 'Actually, he is in Gulmarg.'

I was taken aback by this revelation and couldn't help but exclaim, 'Oh no,' while hiding my face in embarrassment.

Manoj quickly assured me, 'Don't worry, bhabhi ji. Captain Sreesanth is heading to Gulmarg today, so I'll inform him to bring you along.'

I was grateful for his thoughtfulness and expressed my gratitude, 'So thoughtful of you.'

He encouraged me to enter the premises and said, 'Please enter. I'll ensure it's all legal.'

I was relieved but couldn't help but ask, 'Will it be legal?' after being stopped earlier.

Manoj reassured me, 'I will handle it. You just need to get checked out.'

I agreed and allowed the female officer to check my luggage. Once everything was cleared, I was granted entry.

Manoj kindly said, 'Please don't mind, this is our duty.'

I replied with understanding, 'No, absolutely not.' The journey to meet Vikrant was back on track, thanks to Manoj's assistance and Vikrant's connections.

I walked in and begin learning more about the Army HQ. The headquarters' interior was created to meet all of the requirements of the Para SF soldiers, including housing, management, and training. Modern training facilities included offices, barracks, and mess rooms in addition to a shooting range and obstacle courses. A high degree of security was also present at the headquarters, which had access control and surveillance cameras in place to safeguard the soldiers and their gear. I questioned, 'Where are we going?'

'I'll show you a place to relax so you can wait till Captain Sreesanth is prepared to leave,' he said. I walked in the room. The room was compact but tidy and spotless. I put my bags in the corner and sat on the bed.

I heard the pounding at the door which woke me up. I let the door open.

'I'm Captain Sreesanth, hello ma'am.' I said 'yes' when Manoj asked if I wanted to accompany you towards Gulmarg.

'So let's get going,' I said, picking up my bags. I was 300 kilometres from Gulmarg. So my trip would take nine hours.

I muttered, 'More 9 hours until I meet my boyfriend.'

'What, ma'am?' It was humiliating, I said, 'No nothing.' We were moving forward. Because I wanted to learn more about the location, I chose a window spot. Awe-inspiringly gorgeous Kashmir, also known as the 'Paradise on Earth,' is situated in the far north of India. The region is well known for its picturesque views, undulating hills, verdant woods, snow-capped mountains, and serene lakes. The valley was dotted with charming cities and villages that were encircled by orchards and terraced fields. The roadways had sharp drops on either side and were winding and narrow. I was treated to breath-taking views of the nearby mountains and valleys as the bus ascended higher and higher.

Although the trip was lengthy, the breath-taking landscape we passed through kept me entertained. Small towns and villages we passed through had residents going about their everyday lives. As far as the eye could see, tall trees and acres of colourful flowers could be seen.

The air grew crisper and colder as we drew closer to Gulmarg. We were nearing our location when I spotted the Himalayan mountains' snow-capped peaks in the distance. When I closed my eyes, I dozed off.

...

GULMARG,

'Ma'am, get up. We have arrived in Gulmarg,' a voice said. He was Captain Sreesanth.

'Oh, sorry.'

'It's all right, ma'am.'

We finally made it to Gulmarg, a breathtakingly gorgeous valley encircled by towering mountains. My eyes glowed at the scene. Captain Sreesanth helped me carry my luggage and said, 'Let's go, ma'am.'

'Thank you.'

‘My pleasure, Ma’am,’ he kindly replied. We got to the army camp. Captain Sreesanth commanded, ‘Wait here, mam.’ He ran across another soldier and struck up a conversation with him. He returned to me once more.

‘He is Rithvik, Ma’am. You’ll be taken to Major Vikrant by him. You keep your luggage here. I’ll instruct someone to maintain it in the proper location.’ I expressed my gratitude to Captain Sreesanth. He was a big assistance.

‘We should leave, Ma’am,’ Rithvik replied. I went after him. I was merely scanning the area to try to capture the beauty of Gulmarg in my mind’s eye.

Rithvik replied, pointing at Vikrant, ‘There he is.’ His uniform was on. He wore a camouflage combat outfit, black combat boots, and a load-bearing equipment belt as part of his uniform, which also included a brown beret with the Para Commando symbol. The Para Commando costume is a representation of the elite rank of these soldiers, who go through extensive training and encounter difficult situations on a regular basis. These soldiers’ pride and dedication can be seen in their uniforms, which represents their constant readiness to protect and serve their country and its people. He held a binocular in his right hand and a Tar-21 rifle in his left.

With a playful grin on his face, Rithvik answered, ‘You meet him, ma’am, I’ll go.’ I approached Vikrant in silence and gave him a back embrace.

‘Prannnaahh…,’ he said with a sigh. He recognized my touch. ‘Are you here?’

‘I came here to meet you, Vikrant.’ He said nothing at all. He turned to face me and gave me a passionate hug. Tears started to form in my eyes and flow out of my checks. Finally, the wait was over. After waiting for five long months, I finally met him. I was holding him.

‘Why Prano?’

‘I have no idea. I just wanted to meet you.’ After a brief pause, he said, ‘I love you so much, Prano.’

'I also love you.'

'Come along, I'll introduce you to my senior,' he said.

I got to know Vikrant's peers, elders, and commanding officer. I was overjoyed to finally meet them. Captain Manish, Vikrant's closest friend, was also present; in fact, it was thanks to Captain Manish that I learned the meaning of true love.

In Vikrant's room, I walked in. As anticipated, everything was orderly and clean at their home. 'Here, you can relax,' said Vikrant.

I cried out, 'Vikrant, I have to tell you something. It is significant,' I said. He seated next to me while supporting my head.

'What's going on, Prano?'

'You know Sid?'

'Yes, that's your team leader. Right, and he was present at Nimrit's wedding as well.'

'Yes,'

'What about him?'

'He proposed to me a few days ago,'

'What?'

'Yes. I told him I didn't like him,'

'Good. So tell me, what is troubling you right now.'

'I love you. I want to get married to you as quickly as I can. Such behaviour aggravates me. I'd like to move in with you. I want to be by your side.' My face was touched by Vikrant's fingers. He said, 'I can comprehend you,' trying calming me down.

I replied, removing his hand from my face, 'No you not Vikrant.' For some time, we were both quiet.

'I need to get to work. When I return, we'll resume. Till that point, relax.' I remained silent. He went. After a short while, a woman carrying my luggage entered the apartment. After thanking her, I climbed into bed. As I glanced around the room, my eyes fell upon a diary resting on the table. My curiosity got the better of me, and I picked it up to examine it. On the hardcover of the diary, I noticed the name "PRANALI" neatly written. Intrigued, I couldn't resist the urge to open it and began reading from the first page.

"Hey, it's Vikrant Shergil. Major Vikrant Shergil, actually. I am in Kashmir, and after a tragic day, I've finally managed to carve out a moment for myself. So, here I am, writing this diary entry. To be honest, I've never really been one for keeping a diary. So, why now? Well, when you're in the business of putting your life on the line, you tend to create special memories with special people. Memories you never want to forget. Memories that bring you joy and nostalgia when you think back on them. That's why I've decided to start this diary.

Back when I broke up with my ex because she didn't want me to join the Indian Army, I swore off love. I told myself I'd never let myself fall for another girl again. But then she came into my life. Pranali Sharma – a simple girl with simple dreams from Mumbai. Yet, she had a tremendous impact on my life. She loved me wholeheartedly, cared for me, trusted me, and ultimately made me fall in love all over again. So, I'm determined not to forget a single moment we've spent together. Hence, this diary. Let's get started.

The Siachin mission was a success, and we managed to complete it with minimal losses. We were able to push back the enemy incursions into our territories and even captured two terrorists alive, a significant achievement. What's more, they provided us with valuable information. One crucial piece of intel was that they weren't Pakistani militants but members of the terrorist organization Lashkar-e-Ghazi, led by Maqsood.

After completing the mission, I made my way back to Kolkata. The first thing on my agenda was to meet my dear younger sister, Nimrit. I informed her of my return, and she said she'd bring her roommate along to introduce me.

I thought, 'No big deal.'

My comrades and I arrived in Kolkata early next morning. Captain Manish, Lieutenant Aryan, and I were warmly welcomed at the Army Headquarters. The camaraderie within our team is strong, a bond forged through countless missions and shared experiences. I know I can rely on them in the days to come.

The next day, we started with an orientation session, led by Colonel Sharma. He provided valuable insights into the security situation in that region and the key players we'll be working with. The challenge is clear, and our mission is to maintain peace and security.

We conducted our first reconnaissance mission that afternoon, venturing into the heart of Kolkata. The streets were alive with activity. It's a place filled with vibrant energy, but we must remember that our duty is to safeguard it.

The day concluded with a debriefing session. We discussed our initial findings and started formulating a plan. I'm grateful to have such a dedicated and competent team by my side.

The next evening, after fulfilling all my duties, it was finally time to meet Nimrit. I dressed in a pair of grey trousers and a light pink formal full-sleeved shirt. My golden Sonata watch adorned my left wrist, and I grabbed the keys to my Ciaz before heading to Victoria Garden.

Upon arriving, I noticed Nimrit and her roommate were already there. I removed my sunglasses to get a better look at her roommate, and to my surprise, she was even more stunning than my sister. She had long, wavy hair, almond-shaped, deep black eyes, lips as red as a rose, a cute snub nose, sharp jaw line, and fair, milky skin. She looked like an angel, dressed in a pink top and blue jeans, more beautiful than any angel from heaven.

I approached them. Nimrit said, 'Bhaiyya,' and gave me a tight embrace. I questioned her, 'How are you, Nimmu?'

'I'm good, bhaiyya.' She questioned, 'You?'

'My little baby, I'm just fine,' I said.

She pointed at her roommate and said, 'Bhaiyya meet my friend, Pranali.'

As I approached her, her nervousness was quite noticeable. We greeted each other and then moved to the yard, where we sat down on a couch. Nirmit began sharing details of the past three months, and I reciprocated by explaining the details of my mission. However, what bothered me was Pranali's silence. I had a strong desire to make her open up and learn more about her.

Nimrit excused herself, saying, 'I'll be back in a minute,' and went to where the kids were playing nearby.

'She really likes small children,' I said.

'Aaaaayaa, you're right,' Pranali replied.

'By the way, may I ask you a question?' I inquired.

'Of course,' she replied.

'Why were your hands trembling when we shook hands?'

I regretted instantly for asking that question.

'I've never met a soldier before, you know. And…'

'What ?'

She overheard that.

I repeated my question, this time somewhat curious, 'Heard what?'

'That… you people are completely heartless, lack empathy, and would kill anyone without hesitation.'

I believed she had heard lot of bad things about us soldiers. So I decided to clear all her misconceptions and the rumours she had heard.

I asked her, 'Tell me about yourself.'

'I'm from Andheri, Mumbai. I received employment at the Engineering Company in Kolkata after completing my computer engineering degree at VJTI in Mumbai. I had to relocate from Mumbai to Kolkata as a result. I've resided in Newtown for the last two months, sharing a room with Nimrit. For me, Kolkata metropolis was completely new. But Nimrit was very helpful to me in the beginning.'

'Great,' I exclaimed with a grin. There was a brief stillness.

'Can I have your phone number,' he unexpectedly inquired. I think she was not expecting this from me.

She replied after a brief silence, 'Yes sure. 935905....' And provided me her phone and that's how everything began.

In the stillness of that night, I found myself seated beside my friend, Captain Manish, on the couch. Our conversation turned to the well-being of Nimrit, and Manish inquired about her. I reassured him, 'she is doing fine,' a brief and casual response.

Manish then reminded me of my upcoming meeting with Nimrit's roommate, Pranali, and asked if I had met her. I confirmed, 'Yes, her name is Pranali Sharma.'

However, as I spoke of Pranali, I couldn't help but admit something more. 'But you know what, she is cute,' I remarked, appreciating her charm and presence.

Manish was taken aback by my admission, responding with a surprised, 'What?'

I clarified, 'Yes, she is an attractive girl with beautiful eyes. Passionate and lovely.' There was a pause, and Manish couldn't resist a playful question, 'Can I refer to this as love at first sight?'

I chuckled and replied, 'No, bro, not at all. I am just saying that she is a cute girl, and nothing else.'

Manish continued, 'Yeah, yeah,' but my thoughts remained on Pranali.

Before we concluded our conversation and returned to our respective rooms, I felt compelled to express something more. 'I just feel I want to know her more. I want to make her my friend. That's why I took her phone number,' I declared.

Manish acknowledged, 'She is really special then,' prompting me to question, 'How do you know?'

His response was insightful, 'Because she is the first girl you are referring to as cute. Otherwise, I see you breaking the hearts of thousands of girls by ignoring them.'

We shared a hearty laugh before parting for the night. As I closed my eyes, Pranali's face remained etched in my mind, a thought I couldn't escape. The intrigue and curiosity about her had taken root in my heart.

Pranali.....

❑

CHAPTER 18

Vikrant's Diary

November 2017, Army HQ, Gulmarg

The door was tapped on. I immediately kept diary in my bag. I look inside to see if he was Vikrant. I perched on the chair without saying anything. He advanced in the direction of the chamber. He approached me and put his palms on my cheeks while wearing a civil outfit.

'Still angry?' Vikrant inquired, concern evident in his voice.

I sighed and replied, 'No, I'm not angry anymore.'

'I'm sorry, baby,' his face softened.

'It's all right,' I assured him.

Then, out of the blue, he seized my wrist and said, 'Come with me. I want to show you something.'

I hesitated, saying, 'Sorry Vikrant, but I don't want to go anywhere.'

Vikrant, however, was insistent. He commanded, 'Be silent, and follow me.'

Curiosity got the better of me as I asked, 'Where are we going?'

'Come on,' he said with a playful tone.

'All right, wait.' reluctantly, I muttered.

Vikrant's next request intrigued me even more, 'You must close your eyes first, though.'

'Why do I have to close my eyes?' I questioned.

'No inquiries, just follow my instructions,' he replied. So, I obediently closed my eyes.

Vikrant continued, 'Keep them closed till I say.'

'All right.'

As Vikrant lifted me and started moving, I could sense the chilly air and snow beneath my feet. It was evident that we were ascending a slope, and the frigid temperature made me shiver. After a while, we reached our destination, and as soon as he let go of me, I slowly lowered myself onto the snow-covered ground. The mystery of this surprise weighed heavily on my mind as I anxiously awaited the big revelation.

'Now gently open your eyes,' he whispered in my ear.

I was totally mesmerised when I first opened my eyes. I noticed that candles were organised in the form of a heart "Pranali, I love you. Will you marry me?" was written. My attitude totally changed. I felt better than ever. I listened, 'Pranali,' by Vikrant. I turned to face him. He squatted with his right palm on a ring.

He enquired, 'Will you marry me?' I'll never forget that event. He finally understood how I felt. He finally started taking our relationship seriously.

What was my response? Absolutely, "yes."

We kissed till our spirits merged before he put a ring on my ring finger. The weather was chilly. He had icy cheeks. But had a warm breath. The ideal time to show affection.

...

The next morning when Vikrant left for his duty, I was alone in our room. Vikrant had promised me that when he returns he will take me to explore the Kashmir.

I quickly remembered that it was my opportunity to continue the diary reading. So I removed it from my bag and started reading.

"Our friendship began to grow slowly but steadily. We found ourselves talking every day, and I realized that I was conversing with Pranali more frequently than with Nimrit. Talking to her became a delightful habit.

On the other day, Colonel Sharma, a seasoned officer with a wealth of experience, conducted the briefing. He painted a detailed picture of the security landscape in the city. The challenges are diverse, from organized crime to potential terrorist threats. It was a sobering reminder of the importance of our mission.

We spent the morning scrutinizing intelligence reports and maps. Every piece of information was a puzzle piece that could potentially save lives. Lieutenant Aryan's analytical mind shone through as he made sense of the data, while Major Rajat's tactical insights were invaluable.

In the afternoon, we embarked on a reconnaissance mission. We navigated the intricate streets of Kolkata, blending in with the city's vibrant flow. The people here have a resilience that's both inspiring and humbling.

As the sun set over the Hooghly River, we returned to our base, ready to continue gathering intelligence and planning for the days ahead.

I had just returned to my room and was in the process of freshening up when my phone suddenly buzzed. I quickly picked it up, and to my surprise, it was a call from Pranali.

'Hey Prano, how are you?' I enquired.

She tiredly retorted, 'Not well.'

'What happen?'

She told me the whole tale, concluding, 'Today is really worse.'

'What? So, where are you now?' I questioned.

'Still 2 kilometres away from my apartment.'

I replied, 'Wait there, I'll come get you,'

'No no, there is no need,' she declared.

'Are you sure?' I asked

'Yes'

'Okay then'

After a few moments of silence she questioned ,'Hey, where are you right now?'

'Room. Then why?'

'Will you kindly join me on the terrace?' she requested.

'Okay, but why?

'Come no', she said innocently.

'All right. Just a moment.' I marched towards the terrace. The stars were brilliant. The moon had a distinctive glamour shine.

'Ok, now tell me.'

She enquired, 'Can you see the stars?'

'Yes, they are beautiful, but not more so than you,' I said to flirt with her.

She laughed and said, 'Ha.. ha., joke of the day.'

'No, I'm not joking.'

'Oh, okay. Thank you,' she said.

During our conversation I heard a voice of a guy saying, 'May I drop you?'

Pranali answered him, 'No thanks.'

I heard him urging, 'Come on, I'll drop you.' It was making me uncomfortable.

'What is going on, Prano?'

She told me, 'Hold on a second.'

It got me worried because I thought something might be wrong. We ended our call after I heard her shouting, and that made me even more uneasy. So, I made a decision to go and check on her.

But when I reached the motorway where she was supposed to be, she wasn't there. That raised serious concerns. So, I traveled towards her apartment. When I arrived, I found that the entrance was locked from the outside. That was a clear sign that something was definitely not right.

I contacted my group and asked them to help me find her phone number. They informed me that Pranali was out in the woods, far away from the city. When I got to that location, I noticed an old house. She was inside that house, as my team had informed me.

I tried to open the door, but it was locked from the inside. I had no other option but to break it open. Here's where it gets intense—my instincts told me that as soon as I entered that building, someone might try to attack me from behind. And you know what? My instincts were right.

When I turned around, I saw a man pointing a stick at me. I quickly grabbed that stick and, well, let's just say he tried to fight me. But it was like a warm-up for me. I hit him on the forehead, and he passed out.

One woman was unconscious when I spun around and found her in the corner of the room. I realised she was Pranali when I got near to her. She had a terrible appearance. She had rope ties around your wrists and legs. I was done then. That was enough to bring me to a full simmer. No one can harm Pranali because I am Captain Vikrant Shergil of the Para Commandos. I made that idiot aware that the human body contains 206 bones, all of which can break at once and cause excruciating pain.

After that I brought Pranali to her apartment. While she was unconscious, she was saying, 'Please help me; stay with me,' even though I had already made the decision to leave. I therefore made the decision to remain.

In the morning I narrated the complete story to her. She was still afraid so I decided to take her on a date.

After returning to the Army headquarters, I took a moment to freshen up and then opened my wardrobe. The choice of what to wear left me in a state of confusion. Eventually, I settled on a pink full-sleeved shirt.

With my attire sorted, I headed to Pranali's apartment and gave her a call. Soon, I felt someone place their cold hands on my shoulder, and I turned to see Pranali, looking elegant in a long pink anarkali dress that perfectly matched my shirt. I proposed that we travel on her Scooter, and she agreed.

Our first stop was the theatre to watch the movie "Pixels." Later, we ventured into the Royal Bengal restaurant, where I had the pleasure of indulging in my favourite dish, Chicken Kolhapuri.

As the evening unfolded, we explored the beauty of the Victoria Memorial Museum, and finally, we found a cosy spot on a couch in the garden to relax and enjoy each other's company.

'Can I ask you something?' I asked

'Yes of course'.

'Are you dating anyone?'

'No,' she abruptly retorted.

It made me so happy that I said, 'All right' with a sigh.

'So, any ex?' I inquired once more.

'Yes, I did have one,' she replied. That broke her heart. She narrated me the story how her ex, Shiv cheated on her.

After some time she asked me, 'Do you have any girlfriends?'

'No,' I replied.

'Any ex?' she enquired.

I answered, 'I had one.'

'What happened then?'

I narrated the story of Kriti to her. And I also told her that I am still a virgin.

After enjoying each other's company i returned to HQ.

In the quiet solitude of that night, I found myself deep in thought, sitting alone on the couch, gazing at the state around me. It was a moment of reflection, and my mind couldn't help but wander to Pranali. What was it that set her apart from the rest? Why did I feel an inexplicable urgency to protect her when she was in danger? I would like to believe that I would act the same way for anyone, yet there was an unmistakable personal connection that seemed to transcend mere duty.

Our conversations had a unique quality about them. It wasn't just a friendship; it felt like there was something deeper, something unspoken but profoundly understood. The word "love" fluttered on the edge of my thoughts, but I quickly dismissed it. No need to dwell on that, I told myself. What was undeniable, however, was the depth of feeling I have for her. I didn't want to witness her endure suffering in any form.

Being the partner of a military individual is no simple task. It's a life filled with uncertainty. The concept of consistency seems elusive, and the normal rhythms of life can be disrupted at any moment. My duties often involve high-risk missions, and predicting how much time I can spend with her becomes an exercise in uncertainty.

My mind drifted to my mother, and I remembered how she endured my father's lengthy missions. She would stay up all night, sometimes going days without a proper meal, and tears would flow endlessly. I couldn't bear the thought of Pranali going through the same anguish. What if I embarked on a mission and never returned? It was a haunting possibility I couldn't ignore.

No, I couldn't let Pranali suffer through the trials that military life could bring. I resolved in that quiet moment that I would do everything in my power to protect her, even if it meant keeping a distance. My duty was to safeguard the ones I cared for, and Pranali was no exception."

I again kept the diary in my bag when I heard door knocking.

'Let's go,' said Vikrant pointing towards the army van. I entered it and our journey began.

As I exited the army van, the cool mountain air touched my cheeks. The snow-covered peaks that towered majestically in the distance caught Vikrant's attention as he stood next to me. He appeared to have returned to a location that had great value in his heart because of the mixture of pride and reverence on his face.

He muttered, 'Kashmir,' his voice tinged with yearning. It feels like a different home.

'Pranali, I always wanted to bring you here, to show you the magic of this place,' Vikrant remarked, his eyes glistening with a mixture of happiness and devotion.

I leaned on his shoulder, mesmerised by the peace of the situation. 'Vikrant, it's breath-taking. I can see why you have such a strong attachment to Kashmir.'

He grinned while keeping his eyes on the horizon. 'I spent a lot of time here performing my military responsibilities. Beyond that, though, this location taught me the true meaning of fortitude and the strength of love in the face of catastrophe.'

I turned to him out of a piqued curiosity to learn more about the depths of his ties to this place. 'Let me know, Vikrant. Why did Kashmir move your soul, exactly?'

He inhaled deeply, a range of emotions visible in his eyes. 'Pranali, Kashmir is a place of paradoxes. Although it has experienced instability and conflict, it also possesses a rich culture and unshakeable resiliency. The resilience with which the locals have persevered in the face of hardship has made an imprint on me.' I paid close attention as he spoke, mesmerised. His speech radiated a profound appreciation and a connection to this land that was deeper than the surface.

Vikrant continued, 'Kashmir taught me to appreciate the beauty in the middle of chaos. To take comfort in solitude, to treasure relationships that endure even in the face of uncertainty.' Vikrant firmly and consolingly gripped my hand as the sun sank, spreading a golden glow across the valley. Gratitude and affection could be heard in his voice as he remarked, 'Pranali, being here with you in Kashmir feels like a completion of my journey. You are now a part of my story and the rock that grounds me in the middle of the storms.' I started crying as I realised how deep his remarks were. Not only were we witnesses to Kashmir's beauty, but also to the beauty of our own love, which had grown and flourished in spite of difficulties.

We embraced the core of our relationship at that time, surrounded by the echoes of Kashmir, a love that took power from the land's resiliency and the unbreakable tie we had created. Vikrant and I sat in peace, taking in the magic of Kashmir as the day gave way to darkness and the stars started to adorn the sky. It was a part of our adventure that will live on in our hearts forever. The peace of the area permeated our souls, providing a haven from the tumult of the outside world.

A piece of Kashmir was engraved in our souls as we said goodbye, helping us navigate the upcoming storms. No matter what difficulties we encountered, we were confident that the echoes of this enchanted region would reverberate within us as a reminder of the love we had discovered and the inner strength we possessed.

And so, hand in hand, we embarked on the next chapter of our journey, hearts filled with the echoes of Kashmir, ready to face whatever lay ahead with a renewed sense of purpose and an unwavering steadfast love that would withstand the tests of time.

We returned to the army camps as the sun set, leaving the valley in a warm glow and taking Kashmir's soul within us as a gentle reminder that love, like the mountains that stood tall, could withstand any storm.

❑

CHAPTER 19

The Choice He Made

November 2017, Army Hq, Gulmarg

Vikrant had already left for his duty, and there was a quiet solitude that enveloped me. As I sat up in bed, I contemplated the day ahead.

With no particular tasks or responsibilities on my agenda, I decided to start the day by tending to the simple routines that defined my life in the army. I proceeded to freshen up, embracing the familiarity of this regimented morning ritual. The cool water refreshed my senses, awakening me to the day's possibilities.

The army canteen beckoned, offering a place to satiate my appetite. I enjoyed a hearty breakfast amidst fellow soldiers, the camaraderie in the canteen adding a touch of warmth to the otherwise structured surroundings.

As I finished my meal, my thoughts naturally gravitated towards the diary. Vikrant and I had not yet made any specific plans, leaving me with a sense of openness in my day. It was a quiet morning, and the prospect of delving further into the diary was an inviting one.

With the diary tucked away in my bag, I retrieved it and held it gently in my hands. With the weight of curiosity and anticipation, I opened the diary.

"It was a moment that had taken me by surprise. Pranali had proposed to me, and her words had left me momentarily speechless. I had never anticipated this, even though I cared deeply for her. Her eyes held a mix of vulnerability and affection, and her words were filled with sincerity.

But as she awaited my response, I couldn't immediately say yes. My heart ached to accept her proposal. I loved her, and I could feel the depth of our connection. Yet, a nagging concern kept me from giving an immediate answer. I knew the life of a military person was far from simple, and it would bring significant challenges and uncertainties into her life.

I wanted to shield her from the pain that countless military spouses endured—long periods of separation, uncertainty about my safety, and the emotional toll that came with each deployment. I couldn't bear the thought of her suffering as my mother had when my father was on missions. I couldn't subject Pranali to that kind of life.

So, I did the only thing I could think of. I asked for some time to think it over. Pranali's hopeful expression didn't waver, and she agreed to give me the space I needed.

When I felt really tensed and depressed, I found myself sitting with Captain Manish in the dimly lit room, the weight of my thoughts heavy upon me. I had come to him seeking guidance, seeking answers to the questions that had haunted me since Pranali's unexpected proposal.

With a furrowed brow and a heavy heart, I began to speak, my voice tinged with uncertainty. 'Manish, I need your perspective on something.'

Manish leaned in, a look of concern in his eyes. ‘Of course, Vikrant. What’s on your mind?’

I hesitated for a moment, gathering my thoughts and emotions. This was a decision that would shape my future and, more importantly, Pranali’s. ‘Pranali... She proposed to me,’ I finally admitted.

Manish’s eyes widened in surprise. ‘She did? That’s a big step, Vikrant. What did you say?’

I took a deep breath, the gravity of the situation sinking in. ‘I asked for some time to think about it.’

Manish nodded thoughtfully. ‘I see. And why did you need time to think?’

I began to reveal the turmoil within me. ‘Manish, I care about her deeply. You know that. But I’m concerned about what being with me would mean for her.’

Manish leaned forward, his gaze unwavering. ‘What do you mean?’

I spoke with a sense of unease, my words carefully chosen. ‘The life of a soldier is unpredictable, you know that. Long deployments, dangerous missions, the emotional toll it can take... I don’t want her to suffer like my mother did when my father was away.’

Manish paused, absorbing my words, and then responded thoughtfully, ‘Vikrant, you’re looking out for her well-being, and that’s admirable. But have you considered that she might be willing to face those challenges with you?’

I nodded, my mind flooded with the image of Pranali’s unwavering determination. ‘I have, and I’ve seen her determination. But I still have doubts.’

Manish, ever the supportive friend, offered me a fresh perspective. ‘Vikrant, your concern is valid, but you should also consider that love can be a powerful motivator. Pranali may be willing to make those sacrifices because she loves you and believes in your mission.'

I took a moment to absorb Manish's words, realizing the truth in what he was saying. 'You may have a point. I just want to protect her from the hardships I've seen others go through.'

Manish's gentle and reassuring tone continued to guide me. 'Sometimes, protecting someone means allowing them to make their own choices, even if they are difficult. Pranali should have the opportunity to decide if she's willing to face the challenges with you.'

With a sense of clarity dawning upon me, I nodded. 'You're right, Manish. I've been too focused on what I can control. It's time to give Pranali the choice.'

Manish smiled, his eyes filled with understanding and support. 'Vikrant, love can be unpredictable, just like our missions. Sometimes, taking the risk is worth it.'

I expressed my gratitude for his wisdom, knowing that his guidance had set my path in motion. 'Thanks, Manish. I needed this perspective. I've made up my mind.'

Manish, ever the curious friend, inquired, 'So, what's your decision?'

I spoke with unwavering determination, a newfound sense of purpose in my words. 'I'm going to accept Pranali's proposal. It's time to follow my heart and face the future, no matter what it holds.'

With this newfound clarity, I knew what I had to do. I needed to accept Pranali's proposal and embark on this journey with her, ready to face whatever challenges came our way. My heart had made the choice, and it was time to follow it. I had found the courage to tell Pranali that I loved her and was prepared to be with her, no matter what lay ahead."

My immersion in Vikrant's diary was abruptly interrupted by the sound of the doorbell, a chime that signified his return. I swiftly closed the diary and placed it back into my bag, a sudden flush of anxiety washing over me. I hadn't wanted Vikrant to know that I was delving into the pages of his deeply personal diary.

With the diary now concealed, I moved to the door and greeted Vikrant, hiding any trace of the guilty curiosity that had occupied my moments before his arrival. His presence in the room was comforting, and I quickly regained my composure.

Vikrant, standing at the threshold, had a purposeful look in his eyes. His words were concise, delivered with a sense of urgency. 'We are going out to Kargil,' he informed me.

The mention of Kargil stirred a mixture of emotions within me. It was a place with profound significance, and the prospect of visiting held both anticipation and apprehension. I had come to understand that Vikrant's life was entwined with such missions, each one a testament to his unwavering commitment to duty.

Without delay, we made our way, stepping out of the room and onto a path that would take us on another journey, one that was bound to be filled with challenges and unforeseen twists. Our shared mission awaited us, and we set forth, each step drawing us closer to the unknown but inextricably tied by the unspoken bond we had forged.

As the door closed behind us, the diary remained safely tucked in my bag, a secret world of Vikrant's experiences and thoughts that I would revisit in quieter moments. This new journey was a testament to the ever-changing nature of our lives, and I was prepared to face it, guided by Vikrant's side.

...

The rough terrain spread out in front of us, bearing silent witness to the conflicts fought and the suffering endured. Over the area, a sense of solemnity and awe pervaded the air. As he stood next to me and viewed the sacred ground where the Kargil War had once raged, Vikrant's eyes were filled with a mixture of pride and sorrow.

'This place is where heroes were born, Vikrant said, speaking with a tone of genuine respect. Captain Vikram Batra, a man of unmatched courage and unyielding resolve, was one of them.' My heart was heavy and filled with inspiration as I listened closely, anxious to learn about the brave individual who had made a lasting impression on Vikrant's own military career.

Vikrant went on to say, 'Vikram Batra was known as "Sher Shah" for his brave spirit. He was also known as Vikram Batra. He was the epitome of a warrior, inspiring his men with unyielding resolve and an unrelenting sense of duty.

Vikrant pointed out numerous landmarks as we strolled through the revered grounds; each one held a story of bravery and sacrifice. He talked about the perilous peaks that had been scaled, the valiantly taken enemy positions, and the unyielding spirit that had characterised the warriors who battled here.'

As he told me these tales, Vikrant's voice was tinged with a mixture of reverence and awe. I paid close attention, fascinated by the stories of troops who had overcome obstacles and demonstrated unflinching resilience.

As we explored and thought, Vikrant's dedication to performing his military responsibilities grew stronger. He worked tirelessly to prepare for the trials that lay ahead, pushing both his physical and mental capabilities. My previous nightmare had changed into a source of inspiration, inspiring us to fight to commemorate the sacrifices made by those who came before us.

❑

CHAPTER 20

The Biggest Secret Revealed

November 2017, Army Hq, Gulmarg

As my last day in the picturesque land of Kashmir approached, a sense of bittersweet anticipation filled my heart. I had relished every moment spent in this paradise, from the enchanting landscapes to the serene atmosphere that seemed to cradle my soul. The climatic conditions in Kashmir had left a lasting impression on me, offering a contrast to the hustle and bustle of city life that I was accustomed to.

However, despite the enchantment of Kashmir, I was drawn to another world, a world within the pages of Vikrant's diary. It had become a source of intrigue and fascination for me.

So, on my last day in this land of serene beauty, I made a choice. I decided to spend some time delving into the depths of Vikrant's diary. The breath-taking landscapes and the cool mountain air outside my window couldn't compete with the allure of the uncharted territory that lay within those pages.

I opened the diary and started reading.

"Today was the day I met Pranali's father, Pranav, a day that would change the course of my life. I hadn't anticipated the depth of the revelation that awaited me. When Pranav, Pranali's father, informed me that he wanted to meet in Kolkata, a sense of apprehension welled up within me.

He had requested this meeting, and I couldn't ignore the gravity of the situation. Pranav's request was accompanied by a condition, a condition that added an even deeper layer of complexity to our meeting. He made it explicitly clear that I should not utter a word about this to Pranali, his own daughter, the love of my life.

The weight of that condition hung heavily on my shoulders as I contemplated the upcoming rendezvous. The urgency in his tone hinted at something significant, something that could potentially alter the course of our lives. I couldn't help but wonder about the nature of this meeting, the hidden truths that might be unveiled, and the ramifications it could have on Pranali and me.

While Pranav's intentions remained a mystery, his plea for secrecy underscored the gravity of the situation. I knew that I had to honour his request, even if it meant keeping secrets from the woman I loved more than anything in this world.

We decided to meet in Victoria Garden, a place where the winds whispered secrets, and the lush greenery offered solace to troubled hearts.

Pranav and I sat on a weathered bench, the evening sun casting long shadows. It was a surreal moment, and as we began talking, I realized the enormity of the secret that had been buried beneath layers of time and silence.

Pranav cleared his throat and said, 'Vikrant, there's something I need to tell you, something that Pranali must never know.'

As his words hung in the air, I couldn't help but feel a sense of foreboding. I nodded, urging him to continue.

He began, 'Pranali is not our biological daughter. She's adopted.'

I was taken aback, my mind racing to comprehend the revelation. Pranali, the woman I loved with all my heart, was not their biological child.

Pranav continued, 'In the quietude of our Mumbai home, Anjali and I had built a life filled with love and dreams. Ours was a story painted with the hues of happiness, entwined with the hope of raising a family, watching our children grow, and cherishing the joys of parenthood. Our love story was like many others, born from the simple dreams of an ordinary couple, deeply in love.

'Our world was redefined by a single moment, an unexpected twist of fate. The accident that befell Anjali shattered our lives, leaving us grappling with a harsh reality. My beloved wife, who had always carried the dream of becoming a mother in her heart, was robbed of that chance. The accident left her unable to bear children, and it was a cruel blow to her dreams.

'The pain that consumed Anjali was incomprehensible. Her once-joyful eyes were now veiled by sorrow, and her laughter, once a melody in our home, was silenced by the despair that had gripped her. The scars of the accident were not confined to her body; they had left an indelible imprint on her soul.

'As I stood by her side, I could only offer firm support, but I couldn't mend the wounds that cut deep into her spirit. I witnessed her daily battle with her own body, her struggle to come to terms with the injustice fate had dealt her.

'The pain was a shared burden, one that tested the foundation of our love. The dreams we had woven together, of raising children and experiencing the joy of parenthood, now seemed distant and unattainable. Yet, our love remained steadfast, weathering the storm that life had unleashed upon us.

'In our shared pursuit of a glimmer of happiness, Anjali and I made a life-altering decision—to adopt a child. The day we welcomed Pranali into our lives was a bittersweet moment, marked by both joy and heartache. We became parents, though the knowledge that she was not our biological child was a secret we vowed to carry with us, locked away in our hearts.

'In the quiet hours of the night, Anjali and I would sometimes allow ourselves to wonder about the child we had lost, the child who might have had her eyes or my laughter. Yet, we knew that our greatest gift was Pranali, the child we had chosen to love with all our hearts.'

The gravity of his words sunk in. Pranali, abandoned by her biological parents, had found love and a home with Pranav and Anjali. The weight of the secret they had borne all these years, the love and care they had given her, became painfully evident.

Pranav's voice quivered as he said, 'Vikrant, I'm telling you this because I can't bear the thought of Pranali marrying a soldier. I beg you to break up with her, to spare her the pain and uncertainty that comes with loving a man in uniform.'

As Pranav's words hung heavy in the air, I found myself facing a choice that no one should have to make. The weight of his revelation pressed down on me, and I realized the depth of his love for his daughter, Pranali. It was a love so profound that he was willing to bear the burden of this secret for years, all in an effort to protect her from the tumultuous life that came with loving a soldier.

Pranav's voice quivered, and his eyes betrayed the agony he had endured in silence. The story of Anjali's accident, the loss of their dream of a complete family, and the adoption of Pranali was a testament to the trials they had faced. The pain and heartache they had suffered were etched into every line on Pranav's face.

As I stood there, I realized that Pranav was not making a demand; he was making a heartfelt plea.

He fell at my feet saying, 'Please Vikrant, I beg you. Please break up with my daughter.' I became stunned. It brought tears in my eyes. I brought him on his feet as soon as I gained my consciousness. He begged me to break up with Pranali, not out of spite or resentment, but out of love. He wished to shield his daughter from the uncertainty and challenges that came with being in a relationship with a soldier.

'O…all right…sir,' I said with a heavy heart, wiping my tears. 'I will break up with Pranali.'

His plea made me confront the profound sacrifice he was willing to make for Pranali's happiness. It was a sacrifice born out of love, the kind of love that places a child's well-being above all else. Pranav's revelation was an intimate glimpse into a parent's heart, one that would go to any lengths to ensure their child's happiness and security.

As I grappled with the weight of his words, I knew that a life-altering decision lay before me. It was a choice between the love Pranali and I had found in each other and the selfless love Pranav had for his daughter. The path forward was uncertain, and I needed to decide whether to honour Pranav's request or forge ahead, knowing the challenges that lay ahead for both Pranali and me.

In that moment, I understood the depth of the sacrifice and the complexity of the love that intertwined our lives. The future was far from clear, but one thing was certain: whatever decision I made would shape the destiny of our love.

After a long, painful pause, Pranav added, 'And, Vikrant, promise me that you will never reveal this secret to Pranali. Let her continue to believe that we are her biological parents.'

As I sat there, the weight of Pranav's request pressed upon me. I realized the enormity of the decision that lay ahead. I had to choose between my love for Pranali and the anguish it might bring her, or the selfless act of breaking up with her to spare her from a life of uncertainty and anxiety.

We left the park with heavy hearts, the unspoken decision hanging in the air like an invisible storm cloud.

Back in my room, the suffocating silence enveloped me, a stark contrast to the lively moments Pranali and I had shared just hours ago. I sat alone, the gravity of the situation bearing down on my shoulders, and the weight of my decision feeling like an unshakeable burden.

I knew that what had to be done was far from easy, but it was the only path I could choose to protect Pranali from the heartache that lay ahead. As I picked up my mobile, my fingers trembled as I began to compose the most painful letter of my life—the break-up letter. Each word I typed felt like a dagger to my own heart, but I couldn't allow Pranali to suffer because of the secrets and circumstances that were beyond our control.

The room, once filled with warmth and laughter, now felt cold and desolate, mirroring the void that was growing inside me. I couldn't bear to see the love in Pranali's eyes turn into pain, to be the source of her heartbreak. But I also knew that the love I had for her went beyond the confines of a romantic relationship. It was a love that sought her happiness above all else.

As I finished writing the letter, the mobile seemed to weigh a ton in my hand. I put it down, and the finality of my decision settled in my chest like a leaden burden. The room felt like a prison, and my isolation was a painful reminder of the chasm that was growing between Pranali and me.

I knew, with a heavy heart, that this was the right thing to do, the most selfless act of love I could offer to Pranali. But it didn't make it any less painful. The tears welled up in my eyes, and a profound sadness washed over me, one that I knew would linger long after this moment had passed.

In the midst of my own sorrow, I could only hope that Pranali would find happiness, even if it wasn't with me. I prayed that she would never uncover the secret her parents had kept for so long, a secret that had led to this agonizing decision. I had to believe that in the end, love would prevail, and she would find a path to happiness, even if it wasn't the one we had envisioned together."

The weight of the truth I had just uncovered in Vikrant's diary bore down on me like a heavy burden. The revelation that I was adopted hit me like a tidal wave, washing over me with a rush of emotions I could hardly contain. As I read about my adoption, I couldn't help but reflect on the profound love and care my parents had showered upon me throughout my life. Their unwavering support and the unbreakable bond we shared took on new meaning, and I felt an overwhelming sense of gratitude for the family that had chosen me.

Vikrant's selfless act, his willingness to break up with me at my father's request, showcased a depth of character that was truly exceptional. He had sacrificed his own happiness for my sake, driven by the desire to protect me from the pain and uncertainty that could come with loving a soldier. As I read about his decision, I couldn't help but admire his integrity and selflessness, even if it meant that he had to keep this secret from me.

The emotional turmoil I experienced as I read Vikrant's diary was overwhelming, and tears streamed down my cheeks uncontrollably. The room felt suffused with the intensity of my emotions, as if it couldn't contain the depth of what I felt.

It was at that moment that Vikrant entered the room, and his presence didn't go unnoticed. He saw my tear-streaked face and the diary in my hands, realizing that I had uncovered the secret he had intended to keep hidden - the truth of my adoption. His expression was a mixture of concern and understanding.

Unable to contain my emotions, I stood up and approached him, my heart heavy with the weight of the truth. I couldn't find the words to express the storm of feelings within me, so I did the only thing that felt right in that moment. I embraced him tightly, seeking solace in his comforting presence. The embrace conveyed a multitude of emotions - gratitude, love, understanding, and forgiveness. It was an acknowledgement of the pain he had endured in silence and the depth of his care for me.

He looked into my eyes, holding my hands gently, and said, 'Pranali, you have to promise me one thing. Promise me that you'll never let your parents know that you found out about being adopted.'

My eyes were still wet from the tears I had shed after discovering the truth. I nodded slowly, my voice quivering as I replied, 'I promise, Vikrant. I won't let them know.'

'Thank you, Pranali. It's to spare them from any more pain.'

I squeezed his hands, showing gratitude and understanding. 'I know, Vikrant. I'll keep their secret, just as I'll keep our love.'

A faint smile crossed his lips, and he pulled me into a comforting embrace. 'That's my Pranali, always strong and loving.'

In this moment, wrapped in each other's arms, our unspoken connection grew even stronger. I had uncovered a profound secret, but I had also discovered the unwavering love and support of a man who had always been there for me, even when I didn't fully understand the sacrifices he had made. It was a moment of acceptance and a testament to the enduring bond between us.

❑

CHAPTER 21

The Haunting Dream

December 2017, Newtown, Kolkata

I went back to Kolkata and entered the workplace. I spent 4 days in Gulmarg. The experience was fantastic. We discussed our marriage and living after marriage in great detail. He pledged to talk to my parents about our marriage when he returns to Kolkata in a month. I was overjoyed. I began to notice his absence when I got back to Kolkata. He will be yours in just a few days, I pleaded with my emotions. I learned in the office that Sid had fled the building and was now in America. Thank God.

Jasmine's name was placed on my phone's interface. When I answered the phone, she said, 'Hello Pranali, how are you?'

'How are you?'

'I'm fine, you?'

'Me too, free?'

'Yes, yes,'

She asked, 'How was your meeting with your boyfriend?'

With a sigh, I remarked, 'So gratifying.'

'Ah, I see,' she remarked. 'Can I ask you a question?,' she said.

'Yes.' She asked me how it felt to be a soldier's partner.

'So, being a para commando's partner can be rewarding and difficult at the same time. The quantity of time you will spend apart is one of the most difficult aspects of dating a para commando. Long deployments are common for para commandos, and being so far apart makes it challenging to keep healthy relationships.

'However, it is possible to make the most of the time you do have together and to stay connected even when you are apart. Another challenge of being in a relationship with a para commando is the danger they face on a daily basis. This can be a difficult reality to come to terms with, and it is important to be honest with each other about your fears and concerns.'

'Oh I see. Did you encounter similar difficulties?' I chuckled.

'I can't explain it.'

'Oh, I see,' said Jasmin.

'But you know what? Being reunited with your companion can bring you greater joy than anything else,' I said and chuckled.

…

I discovered myself in a barren, decaying environment with a lonely scenery. It seemed as though the surrounding's very life had been sucked out of the air, which was dense with an unnerving silence. My senses were sharpened and I felt a knot of worry growing in my chest as well as a tangible sense of dread.

I caught a glimpse of a form in the distance that appeared to be all too familiar: a man covered in darkness. Although Vikrant's features were hidden by the dream's veil, I could still clearly feel his presence.

My heart was thumping in my chest as I walked towards him, sending a shudder down my spine. He had a distinct difference that was really frightening. His eyes, which had formerly been warm and kind, were now intense in an alien way, without any trace of feeling or recognition.

'Vikrant?' I spoke a hesitant call, my voice trembled with a mix of terror and perplexity. However, nobody replied. Instead, his shape started to twist and deform, becoming a horrifying countenance. Veins throbbing beneath the surface of his ashen skin. He grinned menacingly, exposing rows of jagged, sharp teeth that appeared to be glowing with an alien light.

My senses were in danger of being overtaken by a wave of panic. I tried to get away from this horrific image by running, but my legs seemed heavy and immobile, as if they were firmly planted. Vikrant, or whichever perverted creature had taken control of his shape, drew nearer with smooth motions that were out of character.

Through the barren terrain, his voice, now twisted and resonant with a terrifying resonance, resounded. His voice was a menacing melody of the night, hissing, 'You shouldn't have come here. You have unleashed powers that are beyond your grasp'.

As his words resounded in my ears, fear seized my heart.

Dark, shadowy beings with eyes gleaming with a malevolence that sent chills down my spine appeared from the depths of the surrounding darkness. They encircled us while whispering strange phrases that felt like they were gnawing at my flesh. In an instant, the forms sprang forward, their hands grasping at me and their touch freezing and paralysing.

Vikrant, or the creature that had captured him, raised his hand. Unbearable agony overwhelmed my senses, threatened to rip me apart, and was so intense that it was impossible to bear. In my need for relief from this suffering, I screamed, my cry piercing the darkness. But the horror had me in its tight grip. Being imprisoned in this atmosphere of dread and sorrow, with my spirit entangled in a maze of bizarre nightmares, seemed to last an eternity.

Just as the darkness was about to swallow me whole, I suddenly startled awake, my body drenched in sweat and my heart beating as if trying to break free of the dream's grip.

Yes, it was a dream.

When I realised it had all been a horrible hallucination, I gasped for air and felt a wave of relief wash over me. But the dream's traces persisted, imprinted in my mind like a terrifying spectre. The feelings of dread, agony, and impending doom persisted in me and wouldn't go away entirely. It took me a few seconds to calm down and tell myself that it was all simply a dream, the result of my overactive imagination.

I couldn't get rid of the lingering disquiet that clung to my thoughts as I lay there, the room bathed in the gentle brightness of the moonlight flowing through the drapes. The nightmare's vividness and the spooky depiction of Vikrant tormented me, leaving me with a queasy feeling that wouldn't go away.

My shaking fingers made their way through the pitch-black nightstand to the phone on the nightstand. My heart yearned for the comfort of Vikrant's voice and the reassuring presence that could allay the residual anxieties from the dream, so I quickly swiped his number into my phone.

His voice replied after a few rings, weary from sleep but full of worry. 'Pranali? Is everything all right?

My voice trembled with a mixture of relief and anxiety as I described the specifics of the terrifying dream, tears welling up in my eyes. With his tenderness-infused voice, Vikrant listened carefully, giving my anxious spirit some small measure of solace.

'Pranali, I'm here.' He told me, 'You're safe,' and the sound of his voice calmed my strained anxieties. 'It was only a dream, the product of your fears, I assure you. I'm sorry it made you nervous.' His statements rang with some feeling of reality, serving as a warning that dreams can be warped projections of our deepest worries. But the lingering anxiety persisted, refusing to be explained away by reason alone.

I mumbled, 'I know, Vikrant,' with lingering undertones of dread in my voice. 'But it felt so genuine, so eerie. It seemed as though I was unable to free myself from a nightmare.' Vikrant's comments were a consoling presence over the phone, and his voice was resonant with empathy.

'Sometimes, Pranali, our thoughts build up the most terrifying fears. But because of your strength, we can overcome any darkness that seeks to cloak our love.' His comforting comments served as an anchor while we spoke, bringing me back to the truth of his unfailing support. A ray of hope that could be seen through the gloom gradually replaced the terror.

After hearing Vikrant's guarantee, the burden of the dream was removed, and a fresh resolve to meet the challenges that lay ahead took its place. The nightmare had shown a level of vulnerability I had been hiding, but it had also acted as a reminder of my inner power and toughness.

I felt tranquil as we said our goodnights to one another. Even though the nightmare's horrors persisted, I would not be defined by them. With the love and backing of the man who held my heart, I would meet them head-on.

The frightening dream's traces gradually vanished from my memory in the days that followed. Even when we were separated by physical distance, Vikrant and I continued to face the difficulties of our individual lives while getting strength from one another's presence.

And as time progressed, I discovered how to let go of the anxiety that had consumed me that fateful evening. The dream reinforced the human spirit's tenacity while simultaneously serving as a reminder of how fleeting life is.

Even our deepest anxieties may be faced, and we can come out the other side stronger. I found comfort in our embrace because I knew that we could overcome any nightmare that attempted to block our way. The eerie dream would endure in my memory for all time as a reminder of the strength of love and our unbreakable spirit.

❑

CHAPTER 22

A Father's Reluctance

February 2018, Newtown, Kolkata

The day of Vikrant's return to Kolkata was marked by eager anticipation. I couldn't contain my excitement as I made my way to the airport to welcome him back into my life. The thought of being reunited with him filled me with joy, and I counted the minutes till he arrived.

When Vikrant stepped off the plane, it was as though time stood still. His presence was a beacon of happiness, and his smile warmed my heart. We embraced, and in that moment, all the days of separation melted away. We were together again, and it was a comforting feeling.

Initially, Vikrant had considered staying in a hotel during his visit. Still, I couldn't bear the thought of having him at a distance, even for a moment longer. I insisted that he move in with me, and he agreed without hesitation. Our love had grown during our time apart, and I was determined to make every moment count while he was back.

Two days later, a significant event took place when Vikrant's parents, Supriya Shergil and Vikram Shergil, arrived in Kolkata. Supriya had dedicated herself to being a loving housewife, while Vikram had served as a retired army commander. This reunion held great significance, for it marked the first time in a long while that they had the opportunity to embrace their beloved son.

It was heart-warming to witness their acceptance of me as their daughter-in-law, a moment filled with warmth and familial love.

My apartment was now graced with the presence of Vikrant's parents, and it felt like a reunion of souls that had been apart for too long. The love we shared continued to grow, not only between Vikrant and me but within this extended family that had formed. Together, we looked forward to creating poignant memories and treasuring the time we had together.

Following a period of cohabitation in Kolkata, we decided to embark on a journey to Mumbai, a city that held a special place in my heart. It was during this trip that I got to know Vikrant's parents even better. They welcomed me with open arms and warmth, accepting me as their future daughter-in-law. Their kindness and acceptance meant the world to me, and it was a sign that our love and relationship were strong and supported by the people who mattered most to Vikrant.

...

MUMBAI,

Vikrant and I arrived in the dream metropolis of Mumbai. Vikrant's parents departed to Rajasthan. My location of birth. Maharashtra's capital and India's commercial hub. When my father, Pranav, first set eyes on me and Vikrant in our home, he was taken aback. The atmosphere was charged with a mixture of anticipation and nervousness. Vikrant's parents had a proposal in mind, one that held the promise of bringing our lives together through marriage. However, my father didn't agree at first.

The room was filled with a palpable tension as we all gathered together, fully aware of the gravity of the moment. It was a defining moment in our lives, a moment where the fate of Vikrant's and my love would be decided. The atmosphere was charged with emotion and anticipation.

Vikrant, understanding the significance of this moment, decided to take the initiative. He turned his gaze to my father, Pranav, and spoke from the depths of his heart. 'Sir,' he began, 'I promise to do everything within my power to make Pranali happy. I will stand by her side through all the ups and downs, and together, we will build a beautiful life filled with love and happiness.'

I knew that I couldn't remain silent. 'Dad,' I spoke up, 'I love Vikrant with all my heart, and I truly believe that he is the one who can make me happy. I'm prepared to embark on this new chapter of my life with him by my side, sharing every moment, every joy, and every challenge.'

My mother, not one to stay on the side-lines, added her voice to our plea, emphasizing the depth of Vikrant's love for me. 'Pranav,' she said, 'Vikrant is a good man, and he genuinely loves our daughter. I've seen the bond between them, and I firmly believe that they deserve a chance at happiness together. Please consider the love they share.'

My father's response was one of cautious contemplation. 'I need time to think,' he stated, not willing to make a hasty decision that could impact our lives so profoundly.

As the days grew closer, I found myself in a situation I had never anticipated. The person I had always believed to be my staunchest supporter and ally in life was now the very person opposing the most important decision I had ever made.

One evening, as the sun cast long shadows across our home, my father and I found ourselves in a tense discussion. The topic of our marriage had become a battleground, and the air was thick with unresolved tension. The room was dimly lit, and I could see the furrows of worry etched deep into my father's face.

'Dad, I understand your concerns, but you have to see the depth of our love,' I pleaded, my voice quivering with a mix of desperation and affection. 'Vikrant is a wonderful man. He loves me deeply, and I love him with all my heart. We can build a meaningful life together.'

My father's response was stern, his gaze unyielding. 'Pranali, my dear, it's not about doubting your feelings for each other. It's about the reality of the life he leads. Vikrant is a soldier, and his duty takes him to the front lines, where danger and uncertainty loom at every corner. I can't bear the thought of you living in constant worry and fear for his safety.'

I knew my father's concerns were rooted in genuine love and protection, but I couldn't let go of my love for Vikrant. I took a deep breath and looked into his eyes, pleading for understanding. 'I know the life of a soldier is challenging, but it's also filled with honour and a sense of duty. Vikrant has dedicated his life to serving our country, and I want to be by his side, supporting him through every trial and triumph.'

The room was filled with a heavy silence, as if the weight of our opposing views hung between us. My mother, who had been a quiet observer of our conversation, finally spoke up. 'Dad, Vikrant is a decent man, and he genuinely loves our daughter. I've seen the strength of their bond, and I believe they deserve a chance at happiness together.'

My father's gaze shifted between the two women in his life. He took a deep breath and spoke with a voice that revealed the conflict within his heart. 'I need time to think, to truly understand the depth of your feelings and the gravity of this decision.'

...

Days turned into nights as our family remained enveloped in a web of uncertainty. My father's deliberations were a torment, not just for me but for Vikrant as well. He had been relentless in his love and unwavering in his determination to make me his wife. He saw a future with me, a life filled with shared dreams and aspirations, and he wouldn't let anything deter him.

During this time of uncertainty, Vikrant was not a mere spectator. He respected my father's concerns and went out of his way to demonstrate his love and commitment. He spent hours speaking to my mother, assuring her of his love and dedication to our family.

As the hours turned into days and my father wrestled with his inner conflict, Vikrant maintained his poise and hope. He believed in the strength of our love and the power of love to conquer all obstacles.

One evening, when the setting sun cast a warm glow over our home, my father finally called for a family meeting. The air was thick with anticipation as we all gathered around. His expression held a mix of weariness and resolution.

He looked at us and said, 'I want what's best for my daughter. If you both are determined to be together and are willing to work towards a happy life, then I will not stand in your way. I agree to your marriage.'

My heart soared with gratitude and relief. My father had seen the sincerity of our love and the deep commitment we shared. He had looked past his concerns and recognized the depth of our connection. Tears welled up in my eyes as I rushed to embrace him, my mother and family following suit.

Vikrant, too, couldn't contain his joy and appreciation. His eyes glistened as he thanked my father, promising to be the husband I deserved and to cherish our love every day of our lives.

It was a moment of unity and celebration, a moment when love triumphed over doubt and uncertainty. We had the blessing we needed to embark on this new chapter of our lives, hand in hand. My father's decision was not just a green light for our marriage; it was a testament to the strength of love and the power of determination in the face of adversity.

❑

CHAPTER 23

Finally, it's Happening

March 2018, Alsisar, Rajasthan

We decided to travel Rajasthan for further talk. Dad was also told by Vikrant that his visit was brief. Dad understood that we had to move quickly for the wedding.

Our journey to Rajasthan was filled with anticipation and excitement. After spending a delightful week in Mumbai, my family and I, along with Vikrant, embarked on a flight to our destination. Little did we know that this trip would bring about a revelation that would forever alter the course of our journey.

As the plane touched down in Rajasthan, we were greeted by a stark contrast from the bustling cities we had left behind. The landscape transformed into the rustic charm of rural Rajasthan. The air was infused with the promise of adventure and discovery, and we were eager to explore this new territory.

Our journey brought us to the town of Alsisar, where we were met with a magnificent sight—a grand mansion. It stood tall and regal, radiating the essence of a bygone era. Its opulence left us in awe as we gazed upon its intricate architecture and lavish surroundings.

I never knew that my boyfriend was so rich.

Entering the mansion through its grand main entrance, we were immediately struck by the sheer grandeur of the interior. The ceilings towered overhead, adorned with ornate designs, and priceless royal tapestries adorned the walls. The heavy wooden furniture was intricately carved, and exotic cutlery graced the dining tables, reflecting the mansion's rich history and heritage.

A housekeeper guided me to my room, where I placed my belongings. My parents were assigned a different suite within the mansion, and I couldn't wait to explore every corner of this captivating place.

The realization that our marriage was finally becoming a reality was a moment of immense joy and anticipation for both our families. My parents and Vikrant's parents had several discussions, deliberations, and heartfelt conversations about our union. These discussions were marked by a sense of unity and shared excitement for our future together.

It was evident that both families were invested in our happiness and understood the depth of our feelings for each other. As they discussed the details of our wedding, from the ceremonies to the preparations, the atmosphere was filled with positive energy and enthusiasm.

With their blessings and support, we embarked on a journey that would lead us to our wedding day, where two families would come together to celebrate the love between Vikrant and me. It was an evocative moment that solidified our commitment to each other and to the families we were about to unite.

A date was chosen. It was planned to take place on March 22, along with all the festivities.

...

12 DAYS BEFORE THE WEDDING DAY :

Vikrant asked me for a walk after dinner.

'Vikrant, I never knew that you are this rich.'

He chuckled and said, 'My grandfather was the biggest businessman in Rajasthan. Dad, however, yearned to enlist. In order to enter the Indian Army, he handed this business to his younger brother, my uncle Virat Shergil.'

'But why didn't you tell me earlier?'

'Firstly, I wanted to marry someone who would only adore Vikrant wearing a soldier's uniform. I therefore kept my true self to myself. And secondly I wanted to surprise you.

'Nimrit was instructed by me to conceal her true identity too. Because I desired a man who would cherish her innocence rather than her property. That person is Shivam.' He clarified my confusion by saying, 'So I agreed to their marriage right away.'

A female reporter's voice on the phone caught our attention as we were just a few steps from a barrier and moving forward. A voice emanated from the watchman's mobile.

"The Pakistani Air Force reportedly carried out an attack on army bases. This assault results in the martyrdom of 27 soldiers." We had only been married for 12 days when the situation on the borderlands became tense.

...

10 DAYS BEFORE THE WEDDING DAY :

I saw Vikrant coming my way as I was lying on the grass, reading a fresh book. He appeared to be extremely joyful. He actually danced over to me. He gave me a tight embrace, and I reciprocated. 'What's going on, Vikrant? You appear to be content. What is the cause?'

While still in my embrace, he said, 'Revenge is taken.'

'Means?'

He said after being freed from my arms, 'Indian troops responded to the previous attack of Pakistani militants by killing their 37 soldiers.'

'Oh really?' I questioned.

'Yes'. Actually, the fact that 37 people perished is not good news, but when the term 'Revenge' is used, it becomes good news. Vikrant's happiness made me joyful, too.

...

ENGAGEMENT DAY,

8 DAYS BEFORE THE WEDDING DAY :

The grandeur of the mansion in Alsisar meant that we didn't require additional rooms to host the pre-marriage rituals. The mansion grounds themselves provided an exquisite backdrop for our engagement ceremony.

Vikrant looked dashing in his navy blue sherwani, complete with matching trousers and traditional Indian shoes. Meanwhile, I donned a vibrant pink lehenga, complemented by intricate neck jewellery, bangles, and dazzling earrings. A traditional Indian bride's appearance wouldn't be complete without a bindi gracefully placed on my forehead.

As the guests began to arrive, Vikrant's family extended a warm and gracious welcome to each one. The air was filled with an air of anticipation and excitement, as we were about to embark on a new chapter of our lives together.

The heart-warming ceremony commenced with the exchange of rings, symbolizing our commitment to one another. Religious leaders presided over the occasion, offering their blessings and prayers to ensure a harmonious and prosperous journey ahead.

As the formalities came to a close, the celebratory spirit was evident in the traditional dance performances that followed. The guests were treated to an array of mesmerizing acts, bringing joy and life to the grand occasion. The engagement ceremony was a beautiful celebration of love, tradition, and the promise of a shared future.

. . .

6 DAYS BEFORE THE WEDDING DAY :

Vikrant tapped on the door as I was dozing off in my room.

'May I enter?'

'Of course.' Vikrant entered the space and perched on the bed next to me.

'What occurred, Vikrant? Why you are looking disturbed?' I questioned.

'The situation at the border is getting more tense every day. The Pakistani government sent 20,000 soldiers to POK. They also received support from Chinese forces, who stationed 5000 soldiers close to Siachen. In addition, they are receiving assistance from terrorist organisations. Prana, this marks the start of a major conflict.' I was unable to respond.

I finally managed to say, after a lengthy pause, 'You should go back to the border.... after our marriage.' He didn't respond; he just nodded.

. . .

5 DAYS BEFORE THE WEDDING DAY :

As Sonal, Pratik, Nimrit, and Shivam arrived at the majestic mansion in Alsisar, they were greeted by the same overwhelming sense of grandeur and opulence that had left me, and my family, in awe. The sight of this splendid setting took their breath away, just as it had done for us.

Pratik and Sonal's reactions were a mix of pure joy and perhaps a hint of envy, and it is easy to understand why. They, like many of us, couldn't help but feel overjoyed for me as their dear friend was embarking on this new journey of love and commitment. The grandeur of the mansion and the occasion was enough to make anyone envious, and perhaps a little wistful, as they shared in the excitement of the upcoming celebrations.

So, their expressions of happiness and perhaps a touch of envy were a natural response to the magnificent setting and the love-filled event that was about to take place. They, too, wished me nothing but the best as I embarked on this new chapter of my life.

...

4 DAYS BEFORE THE WEDDING DAY :

The most beautiful and cherished day in both Vikrant's and my life was the Haldi day. It was a day filled with celebration and joy, and the grand mansion was transformed into a place of festivity and happiness. The entire atmosphere was permeated with the spirit of love and anticipation.

The day began with a vibrant and colourful procession, as relatives and guests gathered to partake in the festivities. The entire mansion was adorned with vibrant decorations, and the air was filled with laughter and the sound of music. It was a day when the walls of the mansion seemed to echo with the joyful dancing and singing of those who had gathered to celebrate our love.

The highlight of the day was the haldi ceremony itself. Traditionally, haldi, or turmeric paste, is applied to the bride and groom to cleanse and purify them before their wedding day. It is not only a beautiful tradition but also a meaningful one. The ceremony began with all my close relatives and guests taking turns applying the haldi paste to my face, symbolizing their blessings and well-wishes for me.

Afterward, they continued to apply the haldi paste to my entire body, ensuring that I was adorned with the yellow hues of turmeric, which is believed to bring good luck and happiness. As the ceremony unfolded, every moment was captured by the cameras, preserving these priceless memories for years to come.

The haldi day was a day of pure joy, love, and celebration, and it left an indelible mark on both Vikrant's and my hearts as we moved closer to our wedding day.

❑

CHAPTER 24

Still Waiting

March 2018, Alsisar, Rajasthan

2 DAYS BEFORE THE WEDDING DAY :

The day of the mehndi ritual arrived. Mehndi had to be applied at night, so I was on the terrace with Nimrit and Sonal for a picture shoot. I imitated the positions Sonal suggested to me. That day, the temperature was extremely high. I noticed Vikrant approaching us. As soon as Sonal and Nimrit saw it, they decided to be nice girls and leave us alone so we could have some privacy. But I sensed Vikrant was having a problem. There was a shadow in his strides. He drew near to me and desperately wished to speak, but was unable to. I could tell he was at tensed.

'What's going on, Vikrant?'

'Actually, I must leave.'

'Where?' I asked in a daze.

'Kashmir, this evening.' My legs slid across the ground. My mouth fell open. I was in utter disbelief. I have no words for how it made me feel. Does he mean it? I was worried about what he meant.

'What? Vikrant, what are you saying?'

'My commanding officer sent me an email asking me to report to Kashmir in two days. Which means I must leave tonight.'

When life sucks, it sucks from every corner possible.

The anticipation leading up to a wedding day is unlike any other, filled with dreams of joy and a future together. It's a time when the couple is immersed in their shared journey and excitement. However, life is known for its unpredictability, and sometimes, the unexpected can strike, testing the strength of that commitment and the love that binds two people together.

In our case, that test came just two days before our scheduled wedding day. It was a moment that cast a heavy shadow over all our carefully laid plans and preparations, leaving us in a state of emotional turmoil and uncertainty. All the joy and excitement we had felt were suddenly put on hold, replaced by a sense of disarray and confusion.

The reporting call that Vikrant received shook us to our core. It was a reminder that real life is not always a fairy tale. It forced us to confront the harsh realities that lay beyond the boundaries of our blissful ignorance or perhaps our conscious denial. The news was a stark reminder of the world outside, where duty and responsibility often take precedence.

My emotions were a tumultuous mix of disappointment, anxiety, and a sense of being adrift. It was an almost surreal experience, and it took a considerable effort to maintain composure and make sense of the situation. At that moment, I felt like time had come to a standstill, as if I were living in a haze of disbelief.

As I grappled with the situation, I reminded myself of the strength of our love and our unwavering commitment to each other. It was a grounding force, reassuring me that we would find a way through this challenging period. Still, words seemed insufficient, and I found myself lost in thought, trying to process the abrupt change of plans.

In such moments of uncertainty and upheaval, love becomes a guiding light. It serves as a reminder that even in the face of adversity, a couple's bond can endure and flourish. While it was a tough pill to swallow, we were determined to face the situation together, drawing strength from our shared love and commitment.

Life often presents us with unexpected challenges, and we can never truly predict when they will occur. What matters most is how we face these challenges as a couple and how we support one another in times of need. In our case, this pivotal moment marked the beginning of a journey filled with uncertainty, but it was also a testament to the strength of our love and our readiness to navigate whatever lay ahead, side by side.

'You ought to go, Vikrant. The nation needs you.' I believe I was fully grown at that time. He fixed his eyes on me. I drew nearer to him and continued to rest my palm on his shoulders.

'Vikrant, I recognise you. I am aware of the difficulties at the boundaries. The nation needs you now more than I do or our family. Therefore, you should help your country without hesitation. Don't worry; I'll take care of this issue. Although I am aware that our relatives won't concur, I will make an effort to control the situation.'

I pretended to smile and said, 'Now you should only concentrate on your missions.' Vikrant gave me a bear hug.

That alone was enough to make me feel out of control. But I managed to restrain myself. I didn't wanted to weep in his presence. He swung around and began to drag his feet. My emotional dam burst, and I began to weep as he started to slowly vanish.

"I didn't try to stop him. Why? Because I was facing an Indian soldier at the moment. And for an Indian soldier the nation is always first."

Our family members attempted to halt him. His choice did not sit well with my parents. We had no other option, though. Vikrant fled because he had to. I experienced disappointment, irritability, and melancholy. But I was also filled with a deep sense of pride at my partner's dedication to serving my nation. Being an Army soldier's girlfriend on the frontier is a difficult, emotional experience, but it's also one that makes you feel proud and admired.

...

Four months had passed.

He used to contact or message me initially to let me know about his good fortune. However, he hasn't phoned or even emailed me in the past 30 days. I made the decision to continue to live with Vikrant's mother since the day after he departed for a mission.

My parents urged me to travel to Mumbai with them. However, I wished to remain with Vikrant's household. Our relations left gradually. Nimrit made the decision to remain with me with Shivam's approval. She was really the only person at that moment who could understand me.

You might feel isolated and alone when an individual who was once a constant in your life leaves. In their absence, you discover that you are left feeling as though life has lost its meaning and purpose. You also struggle to sleep, eat, or concentrate, and you feel depressed, frustrated, and angry. It's important to keep in mind that although loneliness can feel overwhelming and difficult to handle, there are ways to cope with it and ultimately find relief.

❑

CHAPTER 25
Always in My Heart

July 2018, Delhi

I was in Delhi and was waiting outside General Manoj Pandey's office. Actually, two days before my departure, I received a call telling me to travel to Delhi because General Manoj Pandey wished to meet me. I was perplexed. What made him want to meet me? Vikrant was nowhere to be found. Is there a problem with him? There were many inquiries, but the General was the only one who knew the answers.

After waiting for 30 minutes, I noticed a female army commander coming towards me. She wore an olive green military-style shirt, coordinating trousers, black shoes and a peaked hat as her attire. Badges, rank insignia, and other military honours are worn as accessories. She additionally donned a scarf that was the same shade of olive green as her uniform. She appeared very attractive in that outfit.

'Miss Pranali Sharma, are you there?'

‘Yes,’ I replied.

‘I’m Captain Shourya Kumar. I’m here to let you know that General Manoj Pandey wishes to meet with right away. Follow me, then.’ I gave her a gesture before escorting her to General Manoj Pandey’s office. He was focusing on the Indian map that was mounted on a wall. He wore an olive green uniform, which included a tunic and pants that had been meticulously pressed and ironed. The shoulder boards, chest, and sleeves of the uniform were adorned with badges, ribbons, and stars that symbolised the decorations, awards, and promotions that the General had received during his time of service. He wore a peaked cap with a shiny visor and a badge that denotes their position and field of service. A general usually wore glossy black leather shoes.

As soon as he noticed me, he said in a sonorous voice, ‘Miss Pranali, please be seated.’ On a chair, I stood. There was one more army commander in attendance.

‘Captain Swapnil,’ the general declared.

‘Aa... okay,’ I said. I was still baffled as to why he had summoned me here. The general said while seated, ‘I know there are many questions in your mind, but please calmly listen to what Captain Swapnil narrates.’

‘The situation at the frontier escalated rapidly. The joint efforts of Chinese and Pakistani soldiers, coupled with the presence of the militant group Lashkar-e-Ghazi, had made our mission more dangerous than ever. We were faced with concurrent missions, each one more perilous than the last. Major Vikrant, leading Team Delta, bore the weight of the responsibility, and I served as a member under his command.

‘Despite the mounting challenges, Major Vikrant’s intelligence and meticulous planning ensured the successful execution of numerous deadly missions. We managed to accomplish these tasks with minimal difficulty and no significant casualties, a testament to his leadership and the dedication of our team.

‘As the war raged on, we received a glimmer of hope as global pressure forced China to withdraw from the conflict. However, our battle was far from over, as we now had to contend with the Lashkar-e-Ghazi militants and their Pakistani allies.

'In a covert operation, we received critical information about Maqsood, the head of Lashkar-e-Ghazi, and his whereabouts in Turtuk. Our mission was clear: we had to eliminate Maqsood to put an end to this war. The assignment to destroy all Lashkar-e-Ghazi's strongholds and assassinate Maqsood was entrusted to Major Vikrant of the Delta Company.

'Our helicopters touched down in a secure location, and we successfully destroyed three of the militant group's bases. However, the final location, where Maqsood had taken refuge, presented a formidable challenge. We knew that the moment was crucial, but fate had other plans.

'The local militants had learned of our mission and immediately opened fire. We found ourselves taking cover behind bushes, with no other option but to retreat to India. However, Major Vikrant had a different plan in mind. He ordered us to turn back while he alone would proceed to the building where Maqsood still resided.

'We pleaded with him to reconsider, but he was unwavering. With the authority vested in him as our leader, we had no choice but to obey his orders. We swiftly retrieved our helicopters and returned to Indian territory.

'The last glimpse we had of Major Vikrant was a massive explosion that engulfed the structure he had entered to eliminate Maqsood. RAW agents in Pakistan and Pakistani media later reported discovering a charred body, believed to be that of Maqsood. However, there was no trace of Major Vikrant, and he was declared missing.

'Hence, the mission to kill Maqsood is accomplished but the master mind behind this mission, Major Vikrant Shergil is missing,' concluded Captain Swapnil.

'I thought it was important for you to know the reality, so that's why we called you here,' the general said. I was in utter disbelief.

'There are 3 possibilities. One, he must have escaped the explosion but we have no information about him. Two, he may be captured by Pakistani militants though they are refusing it. And third, he must have died during that explosion.'

I lost patience after the General's unexpected response, 'We hope, he must have died.'

'What do you mean? Do you have a mental illness? How can you speak to your own fighter like this?' I said in a rage.

'Shut up Pranali.' Captain Shourya, who was completely silent throughout this discussion, said, 'Behave yourself.'

'Captain Shourya, it's all right.' The general said, 'Miss Pranali, kindly take your seat.' I was offered a cup of water by Captain Shourya. I took a sip. The General took out a Lifafa from a cabinet. I was instructed to open it after he gave it to me. There were some pictures in it. Images of tormented individuals. They were truly dreadful. 'What is this?' I questioned.

'These images show our troops who were captured alive by militants in Pakistan.' I lost all sense when he said, 'If Vikrant is still alive, the same will happen.' I started crying.

Vikrant lied to me. He assured me he would be secure. To him, nothing will transpire. But he went back on his word. Cheater.

I ignored the rules and sprinted outside the house. I put my palms over my forehead. Those images kept flitting through my head.

The moment I heard that my boyfriend, a soldier, had gone MIA (Missing In Action) during his mission, my heart stopped. I felt a crushing weight on my chest, and my mind was consumed with fear and anxiety.

I had no desires. All I desired was for Vikrant to be secure. I wanted my Vikrant back.

PRANALI COMPLETED THE NARRATION.....

...

OCTOBER 2018, CHOUPATTY BEACH, MUMBAI,

A heavy stillness hung in the air as Pranali finished telling Dr. Sameer about her heart-breaking tale on Choupatty Beach. The emotions that had flowed forth during her impassioned confession seemed to be amplified by the sounds of the waves breaking against the coast. Dr. Sameer, who had been paying close attention, looked intently into Pranali's eyes and recognized the suffering she was experiencing.

'She had endured great pain and had still been in pain. But she had still been in excellent mental condition,' thought Dr. Sameer. She had required an understanding person. He had observed Pranali shedding a few tears, which she had then caught on her cheeks. She had still been grinning, though. Dr. Sameer had begun to choose and arrange words as he had spoken.

Dr. Sameer extended his hand and gripped Pranali's hand tenderly with immense compassion. 'Pranali,' he said softly, 'I can't even begin to grasp the intensity of your love for Major Vikrant or the suffering you've gone through waiting for him. I greatly respect you for your unfaltering loyalty and passion in sharing your tale.'

Still moved by Dr. Sameer's generosity, Pranali attempted a shaky smile. I'm grateful, Sameer. I am aware that it is a difficult story to hear.

'Your love for Major Vikrant is something truly extraordinary, and it is obvious that he means the world to you,' added Dr. Sameer. 'I want you to know that, as a friend and someone who actually cares about your wellbeing, I'm available for you at all times'.

Pranali nodded, appreciative of his compassion and assistance. 'You don't know how much I value it, Sameer. It is really important to me'.

'Is what I'm doing right or wrong?' Pranali had abruptly questioned. Before responding, Dr. Sameer had paused to consider his answer.

'I'm not sure. But I believe that if I were in your position, I would have acted similarly,' Pranali nodded.

'This is the epitome of true love. Love without destination,' Dr. Sameer continued. Pranali gave a nod.

'I hope, no, I guarantee that Vikrant is alive and will come back to you.' Dr. Sameer's remarks caused Pranali to actually grin. She believed that he was the only one who could truly comprehend her.

'Remember, you can tell me whenever you need any help or want to share something with me.' Pranali nodded in assent.

They remained seated on Choupatty Beach as the night became darker, finding solace in one another. While Pranali's heart continued to yearn for Major Vikrant to come home, she had also made a friend in Dr. Sameer, who supported her decisions and provided a sympathetic ear when she felt vulnerable. They found comfort in the beauty of the ocean and the strength of friendship as they confronted life's uncertainties and the mysteries of the night together.

❑

Epilogue

November 2018, Newtown, Kolkata

Pranali stood on the rooftop, watching as a sea of stars-like city lights twinkled below.

She had just moved to Kolkata and was ready to get back to work after a lengthy absence. She had been successful in securing an apartment in the same complex where she had previously resided. Even though Pranali was back in her familiar surroundings, the city felt different now, and she was unable to escape the sense of isolation and suffocation that had crept into her heart. She made the decision to ascend to the rooftop of a nearby apartment in quest of solitude, believing that the view of the city would provide her some solace and perspective.

She watched a couple experiencing a memorable moment next to her, immersed in their embrace, as the cool night breeze ruffled her hair. They leaned in to kiss each other tenderly as the air was filled with their laughter and gentle words of devotion.

Pranali felt a terrible sense of loneliness and turned her head away to respect their privacy. Her mind wandered to Vikrant. His sincere pledge to come back to her and the recollection of their final hug flashed before her eyes. Tears began to escape through her eyes and glide on her chicks.

She couldn't help but long for the warmth of Vikrant's arms and the way he held her close while whispering love as she observed the pair sitting next to her. She watched the couple's warm show, and the pain of missing him grew more intense. It served as a vivid reminder of the affection and joy she formerly shared with Vikrant, a love that now seemed ephemeral and unsure.

With a steely resolve in her eyes, Pranali whispered to herself, ‘Vikrant, no matter how long it takes, I know you will come back to me. You’re out there, fighting for our country, and I’ll keep holding onto that hope till the day you return.’

She knew that the path she had chosen, to wait for him against all odds, was a challenging one. But she was determined to make it a journey of growth and purpose. Pranali vowed to herself that in Vikrant’s absence, she would strive to become the best version of herself, both personally and professionally.

‘I’ll make you proud, Vikrant,’ she whispered, her voice filled with determination. ‘I’ll achieve everything we dreamed of together. When you return, you’ll find a stronger, more resilient me, ready to stand by your side.’

Pranali knew that her journey wouldn’t be easy, and there would be moments of doubt and loneliness. But as she looked out at the city below, she drew strength from her resolute love for Vikrant and her commitment to the promise they had made to each other.

❑